ADVANCE PRAISE FOR *NOT THAT KIND OF PLACE*

"No matter how it looks on a postcard, every small town has its secrets. In his enthralling debut novel, *Not That Kind of Place*, Michael Melgaard deftly explores how those secrets can erode the mythology of a place and reveal ultimate truths on their own. Through a richly layered story crafted at a riveting pace, Melgaard exposes the faults of the idyllic snapshot of Canadiana and the collective humanity needed to face tragedy and heal as a community. This novel is at once a compelling mystery and a sharp social critique, bringing the voices of the marginalized to the centre and forcing us to question the power imbalance of any Canadian community." — Waubgeshig Rice, author of *Moon of the Crusted Snow*

"Much more than just an absorbing mystery, *Not That Kind of Place* shines its light beyond the standard coverage of true crime to the depths of deep-rooted societal injustice. A page-turning exploration of what actually goes into making a town what it is." — Iain Reid, author of *I'm Thinking of Ending Things*

PRAISE FOR *PALLBEARING*

"Michael Melgaard's stories are deceptively still on their surfaces, but just below run cross-currents of the darkest human emotions: fear, rage, and love. Melgaard's debut collection features characters in desperate situations, attempting to wrangle a drop of sense out of things while accepting or standing up to their fates. The stories in *Pallbearing* are crisp, ruefully funny, and unsentimental, each one a portrait on a grain of rice. A wonderful debut." — Michael Redhill, Scotiabank Giller Prize–winning author of *Bellevue Squar*

"Melgaard's quiet genius, like so many Canadian short-story writers before him, is in finding remarkable drama in the mundanities that make up an unremarkable life."
— *Quill & Quire*

"These powerful, empathetic stories are about the burdens people carry and the debts they owe — at work and at home, to their friends and family, and sometimes, heaviest of all, to themselves. With remarkable compression and insight, Michael Melgaard cuts straight to the heart of people's lives — in just a few pages I came to know these characters so well they felt like my own neighbours, and I'll remember them for a long time. This is a striking debut by a writer to watch." —Alix Ohlin, Scotiabank Giller Prize–shortlisted author of *Dual Citizens*

"With DNA traces of Raymond Carver and Kent Haruf, Michael Melgaard's *Pallbearing* conjures up a wallop of small-town pathos and dead-end desperation that will leave you shattered. These stories may be deceptively spare in their construction, but they are rich and abundant in their impact." — Michael Christie, Scotiabank Giller Prize–longlisted author of *Greenwood*

"Michael Melgaard does the hardest of things: the poetry of the everyday. Tough, heartbreaking, and astute, these stories move with grace through the margins of society, never condescending, never inauthentic. *Pallbearing* gives voice to the ignored, the invisible, the forgotten, and charges their lives with significance." — Tamas Dobozy, Rogers Writers' Trust Fiction Prize–winning author of *Siege 13*

NOT THAT KIND OF PLACE

Also by Michael Melgaard

Pallbearing

NOT THAT KIND OF PLACE

A NOVEL

MICHAEL MELGAARD

ANANSI

Published in Canada in 2023 and the USA in 2023 by House of Anansi Press Inc.
houseofanansi.com

House of Anansi Press is committed to protecting our natural environment.
This book is made of material from well-managed FSC®-certified forests, recycled
materials, and other controlled sources.

House of Anansi Press is a Global Certified Accessible™ (GCA by Benetech)
publisher. The ebook version of this book meets stringent accessibility standards
and is available to readers with print disabilities.

27 25 24 23 23   1 2 3 4 5

Library and Archives Canada Cataloguing in Publication

Title: Not that kind of place : a novel / Michael Melgaard.
Names: Melgaard, Michael (Fiction author), author.
Identifiers: Canadiana (print) 20220469946 | Canadiana (ebook) 20220469954
ISBN 9781487011178 (softcover) | ISBN 9781487011185 (EPUB)
Subjects: LCGFT: Novels.
Classification: LCC PS8626.E4253 N68 2023 | DDC C813/.6—dc23

Book design: Alysia Shewchuk

*House of Anansi Press is grateful for the privilege to work on and create from the
Traditional Territory of many Nations, including the Anishinabeg, the Wendat, and
the Haudenosaunee, as well as the Treaty Lands of the Mississaugas of the Credit.*

 **Canada Council
for the Arts** **Conseil des Arts
du Canada**

 ONTARIO ARTS COUNCIL
CONSEIL DES ARTS DE L'ONTARIO
an Ontario government agency
un organisme du gouvernement de l'Ontario

With the participation of the Government of Canada
Avec la participation du gouvernement du Canada | Canadä

*We acknowledge for their financial support of our publishing program the Canada
Council for the Arts, the Ontario Arts Council, and the Government of Canada.*

Printed and bound in Canada

MIX
Paper from
responsible sources
FSC
www.fsc.org **FSC® C103567**

NOT THAT KIND OF PLACE

THE DAY DAVID'S SISTER went missing, they caught the bus home from school together. Laura sat in the back with Becky and some other friends, talking over their plans for dry grad. David sat up front, reading. Theirs was the last stop, the bus almost empty by then.

David got off first, followed by John Sherman, who hopped his fence and crossed the field to his house. Laura and Carolyn Murray, who was in her grade and had been their neighbour since kindergarten, got off together. David walked ahead, into the shadow of the mountain they lived at the bottom of. The Shermans' field ended and the forest began. A ditch ran along the grass shoulder. David was too old then to care, but he kept an eye out for frogs out of habit and for something to do. He passed the Murrays' house and came to the Mountain Road turnoff. Their house was on the corner. He hopped over the ditch and walked across the lawn.

In the kitchen, David pulled a box of crackers out of the cupboard and laid them out on a plate, the nine squares making a larger one. He grated cheese and dumped it on the crackers, then melted the works in the microwave. Laura said, "That's so gross," when she came in. David took it into the living room and turned on the TV while she made herself a plate of celery and carrot sticks and sat down on the loveseat.

They only got three channels through their antenna, four if it was overcast. They watched two reruns of *Full House* and then Laura went upstairs to call Becky. David flipped to the channel that showed the previous night's Letterman. He watched the monologue, Top Ten, and first guest, and then at five Laura came down and switched the TV over to the soap opera. The soap took precedence because Laura had to catch her mom up on what had happened when she got home from work at 5:30. Some days David would stay in the living room and switch back to Letterman during commercials to catch a bit of the second guest or music act, but he hadn't recognized either that day, so he went upstairs and read. At six, his mom called him down for dinner.

Their dad pulled in just as they sat down. He was always exactly on time—their mom was firm about him being there for the start of dinner. He came up the side stairs, took off his jacket and said, "Looks good." He sat down.

They passed around bowls and served themselves, and their dad asked how everyone's days were. Laura said "Good," and started talking about her schedule for the rest of the week. They figured out when she could borrow her mom's car and when she would have to be picked up. Then their dad asked David how his day had been.

David said, "Fine."

"Just fine?"

"I don't know. Yeah, fine."

His dad put down his fork and knife, said, "You should sign up for something, like Laura does. An after-school thing. It would do you good to get out."

David stared at his potatoes. His mom said, "Harold..."

"It's just, he needs to get out." Then to David, "You can't just sit up in your room and read that superhero stuff all the time."

"It's not comics."

"What?"

"I haven't read comics in, like, two years."

The conversation died until Laura started talking about yearbook planning. They still had five full-page ads to sell. That weekend, she and Becky planned to go to the businesses that had seemed interested and ask again. This would have to be after her volunteer shift at the hospital on Saturday. She wondered if she could borrow the car for longer that day.

After dinner, Laura went to her room to call Trevor, and David was told to sit at the kitchen table and do his homework. His marks had slipped and he was no longer trusted to do his homework in his room since he'd been caught reading during their study hour. He had argued against this — Laura was, after all, talking on the phone — but his dad always said, "She gets straight As. If her marks slip, she'll be down here, too."

At eight, prime time started. Who got to watch what was determined democratically. David's dad abstained from voting but had overrule power if there was a special or movie he wanted to watch, but that was rare. At eight, he'd usually take out building plans or a newspaper and cover the dining room table with them, working until eleven. David's mom and sister had similar tastes and almost always out-voted David. In September, when new shows came on, there was usually a month of arguments before things settled. By mid-October, the comedies David liked would have been cancelled, or his mom would have ruled a show "too adult" or "too disgusting" to watch — later in life, David would tease his mom about banning *Mr. Bean*, who she found "creepy and unsavoury." Most years, David would end up with a couple of sci-fi shows he could watch on nights when nothing else good was on.

His mom read from the *TV Guide* what was on the three channels they got through their antenna. A documentary on one, a classic movie on another, and two reruns of *Home Improvement*, followed by a new episode of *Home Improvement*, on the third. Laura went for a run during the reruns. David watched and his mom worked on a crossword. His dad looked over a building plan at the table, marking down measurements, and once got up and asked if anyone had seen his ruler.

At nine David's mom shouted up the stairs, "Laura, the new one is starting." And then, during the cold open: "It's on."

When the theme song came on his dad said, "Go get your sister."

"What? No."

"*David.*"

His mom cut off the argument by going to the bottom of the stairs, then up them. She came back down and said, "She's not up there. Did you hear her come home from her run?"

"I don't think so. Did you?"

David didn't know either.

His dad went to the front door. He said, "Her running shoes aren't here."

His mom said, "Maybe she went over to Carolyn's?"

She picked up the phone and dialed. David watched the TV, only half listening to the conversation. "Hi, it's

Barbara. Is Laura over there by any chance?...No, it's just she hasn't come home from her run. We thought she might have popped over...no, I'm sure it's nothing...Thanks, please do. Goodbye." She hung up and said, "She's not there."

His dad said, "Turn that off," and to his mom, "Was she maybe meeting someone else?"

"While she was on a run?"

"Maybe they had an assignment?"

David said, "She's probably making out with Trevor somewhere."

"Turn that off."

"I'll try Trevor's." She took the phone number list off the fridge and dialed Trevor's. Trevor was out; his parents thought with friends but weren't sure. His mom said, "Thanks so much, please call if you hear from Laura." She said, "That must be it."

"Told you!"

"I think I might go take a look outside. Maybe she fell down or something."

"That's a good idea."

"David, come with me."

"I'm watching this."

"*David.*"

"Go with your father. I'll try a few other friends." David turned off the TV.

They went outside. David's dad looked around the

house and shouted "Laura" into the dark and waited. He said, "We'll take the car in case she's hurt."

David's dad put on the high beams and drove slowly up Mountain Road. He told David to shine a flashlight into the woods on the right while he scanned the left. The road climbed through the dark and then levelled out near the entrance to the gravel pit. Two Rottweilers that belonged to the on-site security guard came running at the car, jumping and barking at the chain-link gate that separated them from the road. His dad stopped. The entrance to the pit was lit by street lamps. The graters and gravel trucks all sat quiet. The trailer lights were off and the security guard's truck was gone. David's dad started driving. The road climbed steeply for half a kilometre, trees close to the road on either side with no real shoulder, before it ended at a yellow bar gate that blocked access to the logging road their road turned into. Since Laura had joined the basketball team in grade ten, three nights a week she would jog slowly to the gravel pit, then do a series of sprint reps up to the gate and back.

David's dad turned off the engine at the dead end. He said, "Wait here a minute," and got out. He shone his flashlight into the bush on his side of the car, and then walked into the beams of the headlights. He looked up the logging road beyond the gate. He shouted, "Laura." David jumped at the sudden noise. They both waited.

He walked to David's side of the car and shone the light into the woods. Shouted "Laura" down there. Then he said, "I'm going to take a look up the road."

David's dad walked around the gate and to the edge of the pool of light from the headlights. The beam of his flashlight swung from side to side and every few feet he'd say "Laura," until that got too quiet to hear and his light disappeared around the curve of the logging road.

David got out of the car and sat on the hood. The cooling engine clicked and dinged under him, then stopped. There wasn't any wind; there wasn't any sound at all, just the woods at night. David looked into the darkness beyond the headlights where his dad's light was no longer visible. The road switchbacked up the mountain a few hundred feet in, turned around and came back to above where they were parked, then switched again and curved right around the mountain, spiralling twice around until the top where there was an old monument, erected at the end of the First World War.

When David was in grade eight, his friend Eric's uncle told them about an abandoned mining town on the next mountain over. He gave the kids directions and they decided to find it. They didn't tell anyone, just set out first thing in the morning with food, their Swiss Army knives, and Derrick's pellet gun. They hiked over the mountain and down an old path that led to a wooden trestle his uncle had said would be there. It crossed the river and followed the old rail track until it disappeared. They kept on through the woods until they got stopped by cliffs, and then went back down to what they thought was the river between the mountains and tried a different route up. It was past lunch before they got to a clear-cut on the side of the mountain. They could see for miles into a valley they had never seen before, the skyline blocked by unrecognizable mountains.

They found a road coming into the clear-cut. It was overgrown and muddy. They followed it for an hour and were relieved when it joined up with a better logging road. But after two hours of walking along that one, arguing over whether or not to take turns, which way was east or west, what the moss on trees meant, they grew panicky. The sun had just set when the road they were on met up with a gravel road that led them, well after dark, to the highway. They walked along it until they hit a gas station and called David's dad from there.

They had ended up practically in the next town, twenty kilometres away. David's dad waited until he'd dropped off Derrick before laying into David, saying how stupid he was to head off like that without telling anyone. When they got home, he pulled out a map of the area and showed David why he was so mad. At any point, if they'd made a wrong turn, they would have ended up in the Crown land that went on for a hundred miles of mountains and creeks and forest, an endless nature that only ended at the ocean on the west coast.

Until that moment, the forest had been a playground. Even lost in it, David hadn't thought anything bad could happen — they would spend a night in the woods and walk out the next day. Looking at the map, he felt the immensity of the nothing all around them for the first time.

The night his sister went missing, he sat on the edge of those woods, under a small pool of light, and felt that immensity press in again.

CHAPTER ONE

DAVID'S VAN SHUDDERED TO a stop. He set the gear to keep it in place and got out. The door stuck; he had to push his shoulder into it to get it to close. Dirt from the door rubbed off onto his suit jacket. He tried to dust it off while he walked to the house.

David lived in his parents' house, in a basement suite he'd moved into after a fight with his dad. Harold hadn't been happy with David's direction in life and had let him know it. David said he was an adult and it was none of his dad's business. Harold said that David lived in his house so it was his business and David said fine, he would find somewhere else to live. He couch-surfed with friends until they got sick of him and then came up with the idea of fixing up the basement and paying rent. That had been fifteen years ago.

The side door led into the sunken in-house garage that took up half the basement. His old amp was in the corner, a broken bass, half a drum kit someone had left behind when they moved a decade earlier. Beer bottles lined the sills of the high windows. Egg cartons nailed to the ceiling for soundproofing had grown heavy with dust and grime. One had fallen since he last cleaned down there. David brought it into the kitchen and put it on top of the garbage pile that rose over the rim of the can. He pulled his tie over his head and threw his blazer on the couch.

David had meant to turn the basement into a proper suite that could be rented to someone else when he moved out. He had installed a sink and counter in his kitchen, but not an oven. He made do with a hotplate and a toaster oven, a beer fridge and a deep freeze. He had more or less finished the bathroom, but the bedroom and living room walls had spots of exposed insulation and wiring. He'd found a pile of fake wood panelling outside an apartment building when he was twenty-four and nailed that onto the studs. The floor was a combination of peeling paste-down linoleum and old rugs. David's dad would say, "You're slower than a real contractor," or "You're doing that fast enough to get a job with the city," or, more bluntly, "How's the suite coming along?" right up until he died a decade ago. After, his mom didn't bother him about fixing the suite up. Or rent.

David rolled up an empty chip bag that he'd left on his coffee table. He placed it back where it came from and watched it slowly uncrinkle, opening itself back up.

His mom's phone rang in the living room above him. He went into the laundry room, which connected to the main house, and then up the split-level staircase, by the front door, and into the living room. He picked it up by the fourth ring.

It was his mom's friend Mary, who lived in Port Alberni and had just seen the obituary shared on Facebook. She was gutted, just gutted, that she had missed the funeral.

David's mom had died on Tuesday. He went to the funeral home the next morning, and, not really knowing what to do or what questions to ask—funeral arrangements were the sort of thing his mom would normally deal with—he'd picked the soonest available date for the service and gone with the funeral director's suggestions. He overpaid for a casket. Used the on-site chapel and officiant. Was sold on a snack tray for after. And he had gone with a template obituary where he only had to fill in the blanks—"It's like a *Mad Lib*," he told the receptionist at the funeral parlour, who nodded solemnly. He'd missed the deadline to publish it in the Wednesday edition of the town's biweekly paper. Outside of notifying family, David had not made any calls. Anyone who saw the obituary Saturday morning only had a couple of hours' notice to get to the funeral.

He told Mary he was sorry and knew she'd wanted to be there and that was enough. She completely understood but was — she searched for a word and repeated *gutted*, just absolutely gutted, all the same. She knew he'd had a lot on his mind and understood, of course, not thinking to call her since she lived out of town, but she really wished she had somehow known, because they had been so close when they worked together. Just so close. And to find out the way she did. She didn't blame David, of course, she just wished she'd somehow known.

When David got her off the phone, he turned off the ringer and tossed the handset down on his mom's couch.

His mom had gotten a new living room set after his dad died. The couch, loveseat, and armchair were all in the same positions the old ones had been in, but were a bit bigger, making the living room seem a bit smaller. The TV was new as well. David had bought her a flat-screen for Christmas a few years before. It sat at the edge of a deep cabinet made to house a TV with a large back. Everything else was more or less unchanged. The trinket shelf with odd things picked up over the years;

a ceramic frog from his parents' honeymoon; an old spinning clock in a glass case that had been inherited. His great-grandmother's collection of spoons with each provincial crest, mounted on a map of Canada. Except for a photo of David standing in front of the Walmart he worked at in his vest, none of the photos were newer than fifteen years. His parents' wedding photos. Aunts and uncles, grandparents. A last photo of all four of his family together. And his sister's graduation photo — her in robe and gown, the diploma she never actually received held across her lap — hung above the mantel of the never-used fireplace. It occurred to David, for the first time since his mom died, that all this was his now.

The light on top of the phone started blinking. David watched the light pulse four times, and thought he heard a faint noise starting and stopping in sync with it — a kind of buzzing vibration, barely there. The light stopped and the house went silent. His sigh was interrupted by a loud beep behind him, and then a *chunk* noise as the tape wheels on his mom's answering machine rolled into action.

She had refused to switch to voice mail. "It's stupid to pay for something new when I have an answering machine that works just fine," she said. "And besides, with the machine I can hear who's leaving a message." David had given up trying to change her mind, and when the tiny tapes wore out and she was shocked that they were no longer carried at RadioShack, a store he had to remind her no longer existed, David ordered a box of them off Amazon so she could keep using her machine.

His mom's voice crackled out of the speakers. "Hello. You have reached the McPherson residence. We're unable to come to the phone right now. Please leave a message after the beep." This was followed by a second, very loud beep. Her hearing had been getting bad for years.

A man's voice came from the speaker. "Hi, Margaret, it's James Moore. I just wanted to confirm that I'd be in Griffiths between March twenty-first and twenty-sixth, and I was also hoping to get the numbers of some of Laura's friends from you. A few of the names and numbers you gave me didn't go anywhere—I'm wondering if they maybe got married and their last names changed? Anyways, I'll try calling again tomorrow, and I'm always available by email."

The tape stopped. The machine let out another loud beep.

David picked up the answering machine and searched for the volume dial. He turned it all the way down and put the machine back on the little table beside the couch. A few minutes later, he heard the distant, buzzing vibration and then the answering machine clicked to life again. His mom's voice began, "Hello.

You have reached—" David unplugged the machine. And then the portable charger. He took the handset, opened it, popped the battery out, and put the phone and battery in the little drawer under the answering machine where his mom kept her address book.

The buzzing vibration started again. David turned on the TV to drown it out.

CHAPTER TWO

THREE DAYS AFTER LAURA went missing, her Discman was found on a logging road on the far side of the mountain. Reporters came to Griffiths to cover the story of a pretty blond girl from a good family who got straight As, who volunteered at an old-folks' home, who candy-striped at the hospital, who captained her basketball and volleyball teams, and who was certainly not going to be found alive.

David's house became the centre of the search, both because it gave easy access to the logging roads and because his parents wanted to be involved. For ten days, reporters and their satellite trucks parked across the street to film the searchers getting coffee and looking over maps each morning before heading up in crew buses and work crummies loaned out by the logging companies volunteering their time to help with the search.

A photo of David's dad carrying the stretcher with Laura's tarp-covered body across a clearing won a number of awards.

The murder remained unsolved and the story stuck around and became part of the shared consciousness of the province. Laura's graduation portrait was as recognizable as the photo of the toddler in Victoria who went missing decades earlier, or the undetailed police sketch of the man who had murdered a mother of four in Nanaimo and disappeared without a trace. On the major anniversaries of Laura's death, the media ran stories about it; long articles appeared nationally along with five-minute news segments on the CBC.

In those years, David's uncle spoke for the family. Any time a reporter called their house or showed up or sent a letter, it was sent to him, and he'd answer their questions while saying it was too much for the family to deal with. They had mostly left David alone until right before the tenth anniversary, when David got a message on his then-new Facebook. A reporter posted on David's wall that he was hoping to connect, ask him some questions. David ignored it. A DM came a few days later. He set his account to private. Two different requests to follow came. He deactivated his account.

Every few years it happened again. He had learned to keep his social media accounts locked, but sometimes they would get his email. Find his private Instagram. His Twitter. DMs, friend requests from people who, once googled, turned out to be reporters.

For the fifteenth anniversary, Laura's murder was featured on a true crime show called *Not That Kind of Place: Murder in a Small Town*. David's mom had agreed to be interviewed for the first time—the uncle had died a few years before. The show made the case that Greg Dykma, the security guard who lived in a trailer at the gravel pit, was the murderer. This had been a rumour at the time. David had thought his mom and dad believed it, but it never made much sense to David—they'd been neighbours for years. The show had renewed interest in the case. There were more articles and then podcasts.

A couple of years later a girl in Nanaimo had friended him on Facebook; she seemed the right age to be someone from high school he'd forgotten, so he accepted it without checking on her. He immediately got a DM—she was the host of a podcast on true crime stories of the island and was hoping to speak to him. He blocked her, as he did everyone else. He had nothing to add and didn't see the point of another family member saying it was a sad thing that had happened.

And then a few months ago, with the twentieth anniversary coming up, David had gotten an email from a reporter named James Moore. He thought they must have an alert for these sorts of things. He deleted it and blocked the address.

David had fallen asleep on his mom's couch the night after her funeral. When the buzzing noise woke him up the next morning, he checked to make sure the phone was still unplugged, wondered, briefly, what was causing it, and then turned the TV on to drown it out again.

The morning news from Victoria came on. The anchor was saying some residents were getting tired of a dangerous crosswalk. A local man appeared on screen standing with the crosswalk in the background. He said, "People are driving too fast. I'm afraid someone will get hurt and the police won't do anything about it. So, I put up these signs." The camera panned across a series of signs nailed to telephone poles that said SLOWDOWN and CROSSWALK AHEAD. "And then," he said, "the city tells me they have to come down? I'm the only one doing anything about it and I'm the problem?" A police officer appeared on screen and said no one had been hurt at the crosswalk, but they were aware of the complaints. "That doesn't mean you can put up signs wherever you want. It's a distraction to drivers." David went into the kitchen to find breakfast.

His mom had been on a keto diet before she died and there wasn't a lot of food David wanted to eat in the kitchen. He never kept more than a day's worth of food in his mini fridge downstairs, and he had eaten all of it between his mom's death and funeral. He made do with yogurt and a low-carb granola bar. His mom had switched from coffee to tea a few years before, but he found a large tin of Folgers in the back of the pantry and the coffee maker under the sink. He ate and watched TV. When the news ended, he flipped around.

David's mom only had basic cable. He thought about getting his laptop or phone from downstairs, but it seemed like too much effort and eventually he found something familiar: the show that had been *Live with Regis and Kathie Lee* but now had neither Regis nor Kathie Lee. He'd watched the old show when he was home sick from school. He'd liked Regis's screaming enthusiasm, and the way he and Kathie Lee needled their producer, who uncomfortably shrugged any time the camera turned to him for a reaction. They had a segment that taught him more American geography than he'd ever learned at school—people would call in and Regis would put a pin on a map of the United States to mark where the call had come from: Tulsa, Cambridge Springs, Boise. The new hosts were not as good. He didn't know any of the guests.

The Price Is Right, also with a new host, came on after. He got used to that quicker; the sets were the same, the contestants just as enthusiastic. At eleven, he found the sci-fi channel, which was re-airing old episodes of *Star Trek*, starting with the original series and then moving through the follow-up series. By the end of the one with the guy from *Quantum Leap*, David realized he was hungry. He had a couple of keto bars and fruit and went back to the TV. His mom's soap was on. He hadn't seen it in twenty years and was surprised how many of the old people were still on it. They had looked ancient when he was fifteen; now they looked properly old. The show was mostly about their kids; one had opened a coffee shop but was hatching a plan to get control of the perfume company. The same old story. After that, the news, *Wheel, Jeopardy*, and sitcoms. He ate a little more. He watched the late-night shows. All of his hosts had retired. He sometimes watched the new guys on YouTube, but had never sat through a full episode. The pacing was different than when he'd watched Letterman and Conan. The jokes quicker, funnier. Less downtime. The bad guests were given more to do — rather than a dull interview, they played games. He didn't know the musical guests. At 12:30, he turned off the TV and fell asleep on the couch.

The buzzing noise again woke him the next morning. And again he turned on the TV to drown it out.

David had been streaming TV for years, watching what he wanted, when he wanted to. Now he fell into a schedule that revolved around his mom's basic cable.

The shows gave his days structure while he avoided doing anything. He gravitated toward familiar sitcoms on the retro channel, old sci-fi. He didn't leave the main floor of the house. The basement had his phone and the inevitable messages from work—they'd told him to take all the time he needed; he took them at their word. He stayed on the couch, turning off the TV when the infomercials started, and waking up to the buzz the next morning.

His mom's keto bars ran out the next day. He found some pasta and some frozen meals. By day five, David was down to spices and dried legumes he didn't know how to prepare. He ate some pickles out of a jar and ignored the buzzing noise and then remembered the earthquake stash.

His mom had always worried about the Big One, an earthquake meant to destroy most of the west coast and possibly sink Vancouver Island into the Pacific Ocean. She kept a two-week supply of pasta, sauces, cans of beans, and bottled water in the back of the hall closet. He made a big pot of macaroni and dumped some Ragú in it. He put the leftovers in the fridge and ate it cold for dinner, and then again for breakfast. For lunch, he made a fresh pot. He repeated as necessary.

Ten days after his mother's funeral, he sat down at the kitchen table with a fresh pot of pasta. The evening news came on. The anchor said, "Tonight, a shocking story from a small community an hour north of Victoria." He knew it had to be Griffiths; the town was only ever described in relation to a place people have heard of.

On the screen, a police cruiser blocked a long driveway that cut through an empty field. At the end of it, a house half-hidden by trees. Behind it all, the double bump outline of the mountain David lived at the bottom of. The house on screen was somewhere east of David, in the farmland around Bradey's Lake.

"A warning," the anchor went on, "the following story contains details some viewers may find disturbing."

A woman had, allegedly, been confined in the house and assaulted. On the third day of her captivity, she'd begged to have a shower and escaped through the bathroom window. She ran across the fields to where a contractor was renovating a neighbour's house. The report cut to an interview with the contractor, John, full name withheld.

David recognized him. It was John Dugan, a regular at the Walmart David worked at.

John said he thought the woman was wearing a Halloween mask, she was so beat up. She told him she had to get away and to please help her. She told him she'd been locked up to teach her a lesson and that she didn't want the police involved. She just wanted to get out of there. John got her into his truck and then went inside to get a towel to clean her up. He called the police, who met them on the road into town.

John told the reporter he couldn't believe anything like that would happen here. It wasn't that sort of place.

The anchor segued to a story about a Victoria homeowner who was tired of homeless people congregating in a nearby park and had taken matters into his own hands. David grabbed the remote and turned off the TV. In the silence that followed, the buzzing started again.

CHAPTER THREE

DAVID STOOD AT THE bottom of the stairs, looking up. He thought the noise might be coming from up there. He hadn't been able to decide if it was more a buzzing or a grinding, but either way, it had been getting more and more on his nerves. It woke him up in the morning, just loud enough that he was never sure if it had just started or if he'd been hearing it for a minute without knowing. Sometimes he would catch it in the short silences between TV commercials, or while he stared at his pasta spinning in the microwave. He was sure it had something to do with the phone—when the house was silent, he could hear it repeat four or five times with a pause of a few seconds between—and had checked, several times, to see that the battery was still removed from the

29

phone handset. He'd looked in all the rooms on the main floor and had stood at the bottom of the stairs one night, listening for it, but it hadn't recurred then. And now, he waited again, at the bottom of the stairs, hesitating.

He had been upstairs only three times since he moved to the basement. The first was to help his dad move an old chest down to the car; they'd argued about grip and angles and not spoken for months after, as they hadn't spoken for months before. The second time was to confirm for his mom that his dad was dead. The third had been two weeks before. He had followed the paramedics and the gurney out of his mom's room and hadn't turned off the light; a faint glow framed the top of the stairs, showing the imprint from the stretcher wheels on the stairway carpet.

The noise started again. It sounded more like it was coming from somewhere in the kitchen. By the time he got there, it had stopped. He waited. It didn't restart. He opened a cupboard and took out a stack of Tupperware without lids and a strainer and started shifting things around. He considered a hand blender for a minute, but turned up nothing that could make a noise. He waited again, still and listening, for the noise to start.

The sound of the house, quiet now after two weeks of TV, rose. The hum of the fridge. The click of the baseboard heater. And then the sound of a car, taking the corner from Sherman onto Mountain Road.

David watched from the kitchen — through the big bay window in the living room, across the lawn, across the ditch — the car park in front of his house. A man got out, looked down at the phone in his hand. His clothes were fitted and sharp, his hair was up, off his forehead. David realized it had to be the reporter who'd left the message at the same time as the reporter shaded his eyes and looked at the house.

It was dusk, David hadn't turned any lights on, and the angle was wrong for the reporter to see David so far back in the house, but he ducked behind the counter anyways. The buzzing noise, which David decided definitely was more of a grinding noise, started again. David looked at the cupboard he thought the noise was coming from, then stuck his head up over the counter long enough to see that the reporter had a phone up to his ear. When he took it down, the noise stopped. The reporter pressed the screen and held it up to his ear. The noise started again. David waited a few seconds after it stopped and then peeked over the counter again. The car was there, but not the reporter.

The doorbell rang. Three tones, the second, highest note loud enough to distort the speaker. David waited. The doorbell rang again, and then, a minute later, the mail slot clanked. David watched the clock on the oven go from 6:16 to 6:20 before he looked over the counter again. The car was gone.

31

On the split-level landing, the two ferns on either side of the doorway had turned brown. On top of two weeks' worth of mail, a piece of folded paper opened itself.

David picked up all the mail and put it on the kitchen table. He started with the note, which had been typed and printed out, rather than written.

The author introduced himself as James Moore, a journalist from Toronto. He wrote that he had been in touch with David's mother for several months and was shocked and saddened to hear of her passing. They had only known each other a short time, but he had gained a lot of respect for her, her bravery, and her compassion. He was very sorry to bother David during what he knew had to be a difficult time.

James was writing an article about Laura. He had grown up in Griffiths, he wrote, and remembered Laura's disappearance and the search well; it had affected his family deeply. Since becoming a journalist, he had always thought of writing about the case. He had spoken to David's mother several times to get her blessing. They had conducted several interviews by phone and had scheduled an in-person meeting for that week. She had wanted to share some things she had collected over the years about Laura for use in the article and provide some follow-up answers to things they'd previously talked about. James knew it was a challenging time, and he was sure Laura's death was a difficult subject for David to discuss, but he hoped David would be able to find some time to call him back. He was staying in Victoria, but would be in Griffiths most days to conduct interviews and would be happy to work around David. He would be in town the next day at eleven and would swing by the house again. There was a phone number and an email address.

There were two more letters from James in the mail. The first was addressed to David's mom, the second to him. David opened the one to him and saw it was almost exactly the same as the note he'd just read. David put them in the recycling bin, made a neat stack of the unopened mail, and turned the TV back on.

CHAPTER FOUR

DAVID WOKE UP TO the grinding noise again and turned on the TV to drown it out. He put on coffee and took the pot of cold macaroni and cheese out of the fridge. He sprayed the last of the ketchup on top and ate while watching the news over the counter.

The anchor said there were new details in the shocking confinement case in a small town an hour north of Victoria. The owner of the farm the woman had escaped from had been identified.

A photo of a man in a Lucky Lager hat came on screen. He looked familiar to David in the way everyone in his town did. The anchor said police were searching for Richard "Dick" Sanderson. "Neighbours," the anchor said, "were surprised that their quiet street could be the scene of such a terrible crime."

"Jane, Neighbour" came on the screen. She said Dick kept to himself, but often worked late in his barn. She'd had to file noise complaints a few times, but never thought he'd been up to anything as bad as all this. Another neighbour—no name, just "neighbour" at the bottom of the screen—complained about the nighttime work and wondered what a guy was doing welding at three in the morning? "It's a shock, you know," he said, "a quiet town like this you don't expect things this bad to happen."

David turned off the TV. He opened the fridge and spent some time looking in the still-empty cupboard. He took his mom's shopping list off the fridge door. She had written *butter, mayonnaise,* and *Passion Tango tea.* He tore that page off and wrote *To-Do* at the top. He wrote, *Transfer phone line into my name,* then tore off the page and started again. He wrote *Disconnect landline.* He'd also have to transfer the other bills, which meant he had to figure out his mom's will. He knew she had an accountant—an old family friend—who could help him figure out all that stuff; he had no idea where to even start. He wrote down *Call Janet.* He'd also have to move his things up from the basement and get rid of his mom's stuff. He wrote *Pack* and then *Pick up boxes.* He looked at the clock. It was almost 9:30. He wanted to clear out before the reporter came back, and the boxes seemed like a good excuse.

The smell of the mountain — wet trees, bedrock, dirt — stopped David outside. Spring had started in the two weeks since he'd last been out. The air was wet and heavy, but with warmth. His nose started to run. The grass in the front yard had grown unevenly: long in the low spots, shorter where the last leaves had not been raked up last fall. Weeds were already coming up in the mulched flower beds his mom asked him to take care of each summer, after she planted her bulbs. He walked out into the yard and picked up a large branch, then made a mental note to add *clean up yard* to his list. Their new neighbour complained, often, of their trees growing into his yard.

His van made a grinding noise, but the starter didn't catch. When David was young and broke he'd always waited until the last possible minute to put gas in the tank, often drifting into gas stations on fumes or pushing the last few hundred metres. He'd been making good money for years, but the habit of running it nearly dry had stuck. He had done a lot of unexpected driving right after his mom died and hadn't thought to fill up.

He leaned back on the headrest and rubbed his face, ran his hands through his hair, and then saw his mom's suv.

Her car smelled like gum and perfume. She drove with her purse on the passenger seat. When she took corners, it would tip over and dump the contents.

Gum would end up under the seats, where it would melt, cool, and re-melt until she would ask David to take her car to the coin wash and clean it out. He started the car and rolled down the windows. The digital fuel gauge lit up to a bar under full; she always kept her car over three-quarters of a tank. "I need to know I have a full tank when the Big One hits," she'd say. "We live so far out, who knows how much driving I'll need to do." There were suburbs all around them now. Mountain Road had houses every few hundred feet, and the mountain had become a giant development that went halfway to the summit. But their house had been the only one on their road growing up, and one of three in the area, and the idea that they lived in a remote outpost had always stuck with her.

David drove out to the highway and passed through town. The Walmart had moved into the big-box store mall south of town. There was a liquor store there, a Tim Hortons, and a Costco. The Costco was a big get for Griffiths. David parked in the back employee lot. The loading bay was closed and his keys for the back door were on his key chain, back at the house, so he walked around front and got through the store without seeing anyone he knew until he pushed open the Employees Only door by the bathrooms.

The shift managers had offices on a mezzanine

that overlooked the loading-bay floor. If an employee didn't want to be seen by the bosses, they hid under the mezzanine and kept some work handy in case they heard a door open. Jamie was there, beside a pallet jack loaded with boxes. He stuffed his phone into his vest when David came in, then saw who it was. He said, "Oh shit, David. You back?" He held up his hand.

David reluctantly met the high-five and let his hand be guided through the twists and handshakes that followed. He said, "I'm not back yet. Just wanted to grab a few boxes. I've got to pack some things."

"Oh yeah, your mom. Sorry, man."

"It's okay." Jamie looked at him sadly. David added, "She was old."

"You coming back soon? Randy is being a real hard-dick about everything since you left."

"Me being here or not doesn't really affect the way Randy is."

The door above creaked open and before David could duck under the platform, Randy leaned over the railing above and said, "David, good to see you. You coming up?" His tie dangled in the air between them. Jamie pushed the pallet jack out from under the stairs and said, to David, "Excuse me, I gotta get this to automotive," and then, "Oh, hi, Randy," to Randy.

David said he'd be up in a minute and Randy's tie dragged back over the rail. David said to Jamie, "You know better than to say his name. It summons him."

"Sorry, man. Good luck." He pulled the pallet back under the mezzanine and took out his phone. David went up the stairs.

He had worked at Walmart for twelve years. It was his second job. The first had been at a par-three golf course, a summer job he'd gotten after high school. He mowed the lawns and ran the pro shop, renting wedges and putters to families trying out golf and older guys working on their short game. Other than the early starts it was a good job; he could sober up while mowing the lawns first thing in the morning, then spend the day drinking coffee and reading books while waiting for more golfers to arrive. Every October he got laid off and went on EI. He spent winters "focusing on music." His dad was patient in the years after his sister died, but after a couple of years of this he started telling David taxpayer money shouldn't be paying for David's hobby. This was around the time David ended up in the basement.

The par-three closed down permanently after his fifth year. His EI ran out the next May. David had no savings, so he sold a couple guitars. Then an amp. Then a bass left behind by someone he'd been in a band with years before. Most of the people David played music with had moved away by then. In June, David floated the idea of a temporary stay of rent to his mom. His dad found out his mom had been covering his rent in September. He came downstairs and told David he'd arranged an interview at Walmart with his friend Randy. No screaming. No yelling. He just told David to go there at 10 a.m. the next day for the interview and left.

His years at the golf course qualified David for a job restocking the shelves in the garden section. The shift started at 11 p.m.; David and seven others were locked in the store until the day shift came in at eight the next morning. He didn't mind. He could hang out with friends until the shift started and no one seemed to care if he came in after a couple of beers. Most nights, there was someone drunker.

A lot of people couldn't adjust to night work; there was a high turnover and within a year David was the longest-serving night-shift stocker. When the night manager left, David got his job. A few years later, he asked to be moved to days. The company didn't like to lose the manager of the night shift, since it was hard to find replacements, so David had to give notice before they let him transfer. He was made manager of the garden section — he ordered stock, made sure things were merchandised correctly, and kept track of a small staff of other garden workers. The only thing he asked of his employees was to not do anything that would get David into trouble; otherwise he let them do whatever.

He was never offered or encouraged to apply for any better jobs that came up.

Randy shared his office with the two other day managers and the night manager. Each of them had their own desk drawer to keep personal items in. Randy kept a plaque in his that said "Randolf Kaiser, Manager." It was faced out when David came in.

Randy motioned to the chair David had already sat in. He said, "I'm awful sorry about your mom."

"It's all right. She was old."

Randy nodded as if that was that. He said, "It's good to see you. It's important to get back into your schedule after a thing like that. Routine keeps your mind from dwelling."

David said, "I'm just here to pick up some boxes. I'm packing up my mom's things."

"Moving?"

"Just packing my mom's things."

"Like I said, take all the time you need. All the time you need. But like I said, it's good to get back into a routine. Live your life how you lived it before. The world can't stop when someone dies." David tapped a drum beat on his knees to fill the silence. Randy said, "Should we put you on the schedule for later this week?"

"Let me call in a few days. I got to deal with this packing."

"Of course, of course. Take all the time you need."

Another silence. Randy always kept a professional distance — advice for dealing with employees he'd picked up at the Upper Island Institute of Business, where he'd attained the business management certificate that hung on the wall behind him when it was not stored in his drawer.

David stood up. Randy stood and said, "I should really be getting back to work." He held out his hand, then said, "Oh, I almost forgot..." He opened his drawer and pulled out a stack of pink message slips. "There's been someone looking for you. We tried to call you to let you know, but no one has been picking up."

David flipped through the slips. They were all from the James Moore.

Randy said, "About your mom?"

"My sister, actually."

Randy's eyes darted away from David's. He looked at his keyboard and said, "Take all the time you need."

CHAPTER FIVE

JAMIE PUSHED THE PALLET jack out from under the mezzanine. When he saw it was David coming down the stairs, he said, "Oh, hey," and pulled it back under.

David asked him about boxes for packing. Jamie said he'd unloaded a shipment of light bulbs that morning. He made the size of the boxes with his hands and asked if that would work, and then offered to help David load them into the car. David said, "I wouldn't want to interrupt your work."

Jamie laughed. "We miss you, man."

They went over to the recycling bin and dug out the boxes. Casey, from automotive, came over and asked what was up. Casey had worked there for six months and had been disciplined for being late three times

45

already. David had tried explaining to him that the job was easy if you just checked certain boxes—show up on time, never be seen completely fucking the dog, don't steal. He had asked David what it mattered if he was five minutes late, and David had told him it didn't matter in the greater scheme of the universe, but to the people with too much time on their hands and too little to do in management, it did.

Casey pulled open the loading dock when he found out what they were doing and followed them out. Mornings were pretty slow. David hit the button that popped open the back of the suv. Casey said, "New ride?"

"It was my mom's."

"Oh yeah, shit, I'm sorry."

"She was old."

They loaded the boxes and then watched the back gate lower. Casey said, "Cool," to no one, and then said, "You know, I got a break coming up . . ." He opened his hand to show them a joint in his palm.

"It's kind of early," David said.

"I always smoke up during morning break," Casey said.

David sighed. He knew Jamie smoked before shifts sometimes, but he was better at hiding it. Every time Casey got back from his break he had bloodshot eyes and couldn't focus. David figured it didn't matter if he encouraged it or not; Casey wouldn't be there long. He said, "Why not?"

The smell of his mom's gum and perfume was quickly stifled by the smell of pot. Casey handed David the joint. He took two puffs and coughed; it had been a few years since he'd smoked. He passed the joint to Jamie and turned the key. His mom's pre-sets were all talk radio. He flipped around until he found the classic rock station and then leaned back in the seat.

Casey said he got his pot from the government store. It was better—scientifically engineered to be more potent. Technology, he said, makes the best weed. Jamie thought it was good, but liked to get his from a guy he knew who grew it outdoors. Free-range, organic, more natural. You take into your body what they put into it, he said. The government weed was all chemical fertilizers—Jamie wanted to smoke nature. David tuned them out; he'd had his fill of pot chit-chat in high school.

Pot had always been big business in Griffiths. David's mom would tell him about the hippies coming in the sixties. They thought the West Coast was a perfect place for their utopia; land was cheap, nature everywhere. They started communes in the woods that were really grow-ops. His mom had known some girls who were drawn into "that life." A friend of hers had been arrested with a van full of weed; her boyfriend had gotten her to drive it into town because he thought the police would leave a pretty young girl alone. "Imagine," his mom would say when drugs came up and she thought David needed a scare, "throwing your life away like that."

David found out years later that the woman who had "thrown her life away" was the local MLA. Being a pretty young girl hadn't stopped her from getting arrested, but it did stop her from going to jail. She spun the arrest as activism when she got into politics.

Bikers came to town and got into the pot business in the late sixties. They were aggressive and armed. There was trouble — some hippies went into the woods and were never heard from again, and then the bikers were the only ones doing any large-scale growing.

When the forest industry had some bad years in the eighties, the bikers bought up the small contract businesses — the shake cutting, tree stripping, tree planting companies. It was a good way for them to launder money, and it gave them legal access to the logging roads that led to their crops. And a lot of people who might otherwise have ended up unemployed kept working. People had jobs, the companies stayed locally owned, and some of the bikers turned out to be good employers, too — decent wages and benefits and everything. No one seemed to mind working for them. "Either way, we're working for crooks," they'd say.

The bikers moved most of their operations indoors in the early 2000s. Grow-ops were more reliable, and you didn't need to have some guy camping out in the woods to watch the crops. And they started subcontracting the work. After high school, some guys David knew had their place lit up by the bikers. This was when the bikers took your basement and installed all the gear to grow the pot. Then they'd harvest it and give the renter five thousand bucks for their trouble. There was risk, but the idea was that by the time the hydro company noticed the spike in electricity use and let the cops know, the pot would be out. David had never heard of anyone getting busted.

When pot was legalized, the retired cops the government hired to oversee the distribution hired the old bikers to handle growing. They already had the infrastructure set up and that's just the way things worked in Griffiths.

Which is what Jamie was arguing when "Comfortably Numb" faded out and David tuned back into the conversation. He said, "Aside from the quality of the pot, we have a moral obligation to support local business and keep money out of the hands of retired pigs. It's all corrupt," he said.

"But it's grown locally," Casey said. "The government just takes the tax off. The money goes into roads or whatever."

"'Whatever,'" Jamie said, "is more cops and toys for the cops. The local pigs just got a tank."

"It isn't a tank. It's, like, an armoured truck."

"They had a picture of it in the paper last week. It's a tank," Jamie insisted. "It has one of those spinny gun things on top."

David said, "Turret." Everyone nodded and leaned back in their seats.

Casey said, "Oh shit, man, you hear about that guy with the rape dungeon?"

Jamie said, "He shops here. We brought up his charge account this morning. Dude bought a ton of chains a few weeks ago. And some padlocks."

David caught up with what they were talking about and said, "That Sanderson guy?"

"Yeah, man," Jamie said. "I live out by his house. When I saw it on the news, I checked, but there was nothing under his name. So I looked up his address and found his file. His account is under his mom's name."

"That's some motherfucking csi shit," Casey said.

Jamie told them that Sanderson had moved out to that place about five years before. He'd fixed up the old farmhouse and converted a couple of barns into rental suites. He thought there were maybe seven or eight people living out there. Jamie had no idea how Sanderson could have gotten away with locking some-one up without everyone knowing.

"What about the welding?" Jamie didn't know what David meant. "On the news, a neighbour said he was welding all night."

"He was always up late listening to music in one of his barns. Sound really carries out there. Like, we live a couple kilometres away but can hear it."

Casey said, "Maybe he was building the dungeon."

"I don't know," Jamie said. "But I do know he bought fifty feet of chain, and, like, a hammer and some shit. But the chains seem the most..." They all waited and he came up with "permanent."

"Pertinent," David said. "You tell anyone?"

"I guess I should."

"Tell Randy," David said. "Let him deal with it."

"Right."

Casey said, "But, you know, it's a pretty sweet idea." The others didn't follow.

He said, "Not, like, killing anyone. But, like, a room with a woman in it you can go fuck any time you want. That's pretty cool."

Jamie said, "Dude, what?"

"No, I just mean, like. Fuck. Not like beating her up or anything like that. That's fucked. I mean just, like, there's always a woman around to fuck, she's got to do whatever you want, you know? That'd be awesome."

David said, "I gotta run fellas."

Casey said, "No, I just mean..."

David got out of the car. The other two did the same.

Right after Jamie was hired, he had said to David, "Your sister was the one on the mountain, right?" No one ever came out and said it like that. David could always tell the moment the name clicked — a quick double glance, a sudden look away. Jamie had just blurted it out, and when David told him yes he said, "That sucks, man." David had always appreciated that.

Casey tried to explain himself. Jamie said, "Shut the fuck up, man." David got back into the car.

CHAPTER SIX

THE CAR BEHIND DAVID beeped. He looked in the rear-view mirror and saw the driver's arm out the window, waving forward. David looked ahead, then up. The light was green. He hit the gas and the wheels on the suv squealed; his mom's car was more responsive than his van. He rounded the corner onto the highway, fishtailing slightly before straightening out. Casey was right, he thought, the government weed was more potent. He slowed down and drove toward town.

Cars flew past him on the right. As the highway entered town it turned into a regular road and the speed limit dropped. At the first light, a car pulled up beside David. The driver rolled down the window and held out his middle finger. David looked straight ahead and tapped on the steering wheel, waiting for the light to change.

The downtown of Griffiths had grown around a train station. There had been warehouses, a Hudson's Bay, and a couple of streets of two-storey wooden shops that made up the old downtown, which, except for a few improvements and one three-storey condo on the site of a bar that had burned down in 1978, hadn't changed since its founding. The east of town had originally been a Chinatown; the miners and a lot of forestry workers had been Chinese labourers brought in on the cheap. When that work slowed down in the 1960s, the Chinatown had been demolished to make way for the highway and the gas stations and fast-food places that had gone with it. The old town mall was right off the highway; it was now mostly abandoned, since the businesses had moved out to the new box-store complex. David pulled into the lot and parked to collect himself.

He realized he was hungry. Thought about driving downtown but decided walking was safer. He could clear his head and the town was small anyways; nothing was more than a ten-minute walk from anything else. He left his car. Crossed the parking lot by the Tim Hortons — one of four now along the highway — and then crossed the unused train tracks into the old downtown. The Rainbow Café was on the far side of town, by the old courthouse.

David had started going to the Rainbow the last year of school. His sister had gone missing near the end of grade eleven. By the time it was all done, there were only a couple of weeks of school left. No one fought David when he said he didn't want to go back. None of his friends had called while she was missing and none came to the funeral. That summer he only saw Laura's friends, dropping by to see his mom and dad, and then they left for August — his dad thought he should do something to "get back to normal" and took them all on a road trip to the Rockies and Alberta, where he acted anything but normal. Smiling, forcing fun neither David nor his mom felt like participating in. At the West Edmonton Mall, Harold had tried to get David to the amusement park. David just wanted to buy a book and stay in the room, and for the first time since Laura died, his dad lost his temper. They drove back barely talking, normalcy returning.

The first day of grade twelve, he went to the usual spot he hung out at in the annex building, by the library and computer lab — the Nerd Wing was what everyone called it. After a solid thirty seconds of silence after he came up the stairs, his friends started talking about their summers without asking about his. At lunch that day, David went to the park beside the school where the smokers hung out. A girl he'd had a class with the year before was there. Her hair was cut short and dyed green. She had patches safety-pinned to her oversized green jacket. She said, "Oh shit, how the fuck are you?" and gave him a hug.

Griffiths wasn't big enough to support separate alt-kid scenes, so the three punks, the four goths, the dozen hippies, and the five ravers in the high school all hung out with each other in solidarity. David had been playing guitar for a couple of years. One of the older guys, already graduated, jammed with him and gave him records, and within a few months he'd settled into the new group as their rock-nerd guy. He skipped school to go thrifting and read in cafés. The Rainbow was their main hangout. He spent hours sitting in the back booth, with friends or alone, reading and drinking bottomless coffees and sometimes pooling their money for fries.

Sue ignored David when he walked by the counter. His usual spot in the back booth was open. He sat down and waited. Sue came back and said, "We're still on breakfast, so if you want your usual it'll be a wait."

"I'll wait. Could I get a coffee?"

Sue walked away. She had been working at the Rainbow since David first started going. He hadn't known about tipping in grade twelve — his family didn't eat out much, and when they did, he wasn't paying. It had been nineteen years now he'd been over-tipping to make up for the mistake, but Sue never got friendlier.

His phone was still in his basement suite and he
hadn't brought anything to read. He went to the stack
of newspapers and pulled out the city paper. The
woman who escaped was the cover story, but the article was old already; it didn't know the name of the
guy who had trapped her. He flipped to the next page.
A car had crashed on the mountain highway between
Griffiths and Victoria at the spot where they always
crashed. A divider, a warning light, and a low speed
limit had been added over the years, but there was no
correcting for people ignoring all that. The quoted
traffic officer was clearly exasperated — "People just
need to follow the posted rules." A letter to the editor
complained about the homeless encampments in the
local parks. The author had sympathy, but parks were
meant for public enjoyment, not for camping. If they
needed work, he thought they should all head down to
the mill with their resumés. A pig had gotten loose at
the golf course outside of Fuller's Bay.

David put the paper down. Becky, his sister's best
friend, walked toward him.

BECKY HAD BEEN AT his mom's funeral; she was one of
the people who followed the hearse from the service to
the graveyard. When the priest finished the graveside
rights, David shook hands with him and saw Becky

eyeing him in a small crowd of others. David slipped off into the graves, hoping people would think he was overcome with emotion and disperse.

He'd made his way down the rows, reading the names on the gravestones. He stopped when he saw the name of his middle-school math teacher. David hadn't heard he'd died. He recognized the name of a former mayor, a friend of his dad's who had owned a lighting store in town, the mother of someone he went to high school with. He recognized a lot of last names without knowing who the person was: grandparents of people he knew, based on the dates, or well-known local names. An Atkinson who died in 1944 was probably related to the Atkinson his elementary school had been named after; a Griffiths likely related to the town's founder. Then he read his dad's name, and beside it, his sister's.

A salesman had seen his parents' wedding announcement and was waiting for them after their honeymoon. He sold them plots beside each other. When David's sister died, she was given his mom's spot. His parents tried to buy the empty plot beside his sister, but it was owned by a man who had been predeceased by his wife and who wouldn't even think of being buried elsewhere. His dad had been buried next to Laura and his mom had ended up buying a new plot for herself a few rows away. "Close enough," she'd said, "not that I'll know any better."

David was thinking he should probably look into getting himself a plot when Becky said, behind him, "It's still hard, after all of these years." She stepped beside David, staring at Laura's gravestone. "I wanted to say a few things about your mom. I'd hoped that they'd ask."

David said, "No one ever wants to get up, but they feel like they should."

"Some people feel it's an opportunity to share, to honour, and to mourn together."

David said, "Uh-huh."

"Your mom was always such a big part of my life, you know. She was such a light." Becky had been in junior Toastmasters in high school. David had tried not to sigh as she shifted into presentation mode and he realized he was going to get her speech anyways. Her cadence was prepared, pauses rehearsed. "Your home was like my own when I was young. You know, my parents divorced, my mom wasn't often around. I spent so many nights at your place. You remember, staying up late, playing games, watching movies. I found comfort. Laura was like a sister. You were all like family.

"And then, your sister passed."

She'd stared out over the graveyard in a way David was sure had been noted on her rehearsal script.

"After," she continued, "your mom and I shared our mutual loss and found our family bond was undiminished. Your mom helped me through the pain. She helped me with my marriage, my children. She has been...had been...a rock in my life. A shoulder to cry on. A mentor. A friend. And because she was like a mother, I always thought of you" — she turned to face David — "as a brother. And family should mourn together."

She hugged David. He looked at the clouds blowing around the top of the mountain, over his house. She sniffled and pushed back.

David said, "Yes. It's very sad."

"I know this is a lot for you to talk about right now. But I hope I can come by. Visit with you. Share memories. And," she said importantly, "there are some things I need to talk to you about, too. Can I call you?"

David said, "Any time."

BECKY SAID, "I'VE BEEN trying to call you."

"My phone hasn't been working..."

"And your mom's line too."

"I haven't been picking that one up."

"Well, I'm happy to bump into you. Do you mind?" She pulled her purse across her front and slumped into the booth. She shuffled over and spent a minute untangling her purse from her coat and getting them all in a pile to her side.

Sue came over and asked, "Coffee?"

"Do you have any herbal tea?"

Sue flipped her order pad shut. "I'll check."

"I have had such a hard time getting in touch with you," Becky said. "I popped into your work and they said I just missed you. I happened to see your mom's car by the mall, so thought you must be around somewhere. I'm glad I saw you through the window."

"You were driving around looking for me?"

"I had some things to do in town. I just thought if I saw you..."

"We've got a mint and a green," Sue told Becky, who went with the mint.

David rubbed his eyes with the heel of his hands. Becky said, "Are you all right?"

"Fine, yeah."

"I mean, I know things are hard for you right now. You must be so sad. I have been too."

David realized his eyes must be bloodshot. He said, "Oh, no. I smoked pot for the first time in, like, a decade earlier today."

"I always stayed away from that stuff. I know too many people who got into pot in high school and then ended up doing harder stuff. It's a gateway drug."

"That reminds me, do you know where I can get some heroin? I've got a hankering." Becky had never been good with irony. David added, "I'm joking."

"Well, that's good."

"...I haven't done heroin in years."

Sue put a teapot on the table and asked if Becky wanted anything to eat. Becky wanted to see a menu. Sue rolled her eyes and went to get one from behind the counter. David said, "Sorry about Sue. She kind of hates me."

"Why?"

"I didn't know I was supposed to tip the first few years I came here. I've tried to make up for it, but..."

"Well, a tip should be based on service and she clearly has an attitude, so you shouldn't feel too bad."

David rubbed his eyes again. He said, "How's Trev?"

Becky blinked. She said, "We separated. Trevor moved to Fort Mac. He'd been working there for years anyways." David had known this from his mom. He also knew from his mom that the reason for the move was that Trevor had knocked up a younger woman there. "Some little chick," his mom had said. "You know how they are."

"I'm sorry to hear that," David said.

"It's for the best, I think. I've been coming to grips with a lot of our relationship. Therapy, you know. And reading a lot about codependence. We didn't get together under" — she made a show of trying to find the right term — "ideal circumstances."

Trevor had been dating Laura when she went

missing. Three months after Laura died, he came to the house with Becky. He wore a tie and a dress shirt with creases from the box it came out of. Becky wore what David thought must have been her prom dress. David normally hid in his room when Becky showed up, but this time his mom called him down. His dad had been called in, too. David's mom said, "Becky has asked if she can tell us something,"

Becky had said, in her junior Toastmaster's voice, "Pain can bring people together. Suffering can unify." She quoted something from the Bible and David didn't follow what she was getting at for the first five minutes, and then he realized she was telling them that she and Trevor had started dating and were seeking his family's blessing on the union. Or Becky was seeking; Trevor looked like he'd rather be anywhere else.

David's mom thought it was just fine and she wished them luck. Becky cried and said she knew they'd understand. After they left, David and his dad both sighed at the same time. They looked at each other and laughed. It was the first laugh they'd shared in a long time. Becky had her first baby seven months later.

David said, "What do you need, Becky?"

She laid both hands flat on either side of her placemat. She looked at the table and then up. "I need to talk to you about your sister." She added, "Laura."

"This about the reporter?"

63

"You know about him?"

"This guy has been calling me every five minutes for the last two weeks. He has mailed me letters and shown up at my door. He had the nerve" — David looked at Becky flatly — "to show up at my work looking for me."

Sue said, "You get a chance to look at the menu."

"Oh, not yet. But..." Becky flipped it open and Sue stuck her hip out and put a hand on it. She tapped her pad. Becky said, "The green salad, please."

Sue stared at her until Becky held up the menu. Sue took it and left.

Becky said, "So, you're going to talk with James?"

"If a person is not responding to calls and messages, that usually means they don't want to talk to the person leaving those messages — no."

"I'm partially to blame for James bothering you."

"You don't say."

"James got in touch with me, first. He had seen me interviewed on that documentary, *Not That Kind of Place*. That was so terrible. You know, your mom said she'd never talk to reporters again after that came out?"

"Did she?"

"She never told you?"

David's mom had told him she agreed to the interview. The morning it took place, the sound of people moving things around in the living room had woken

David up. He had left out the side door, a couple of guys were moving lights from a van into the house. A man with a headset and clipboard saw David. He came over and said, "You're the brother, right?" David got into his van and pulled out of the driveway. He didn't watch the show until a year after it came out and someone put it on YouTube.

The episode opened with a brief overview of the case. A missing girl, a worried family, a community coming together. The photo of David's dad with the stretcher appeared, the narrator said, "An end that shocked an idyllic community," and then David's mother appeared on screen saying, "I think about it every day" while picking up a framed photo of Laura and wiping away tears.

The clip of his mom was used a dozen times — before each commercial break, and near the end, when it was added to a second clip where she said, "That man will have to live with what he did, and that is punishment enough." After she said that, a mugshot of their neighbour Greg Dykma came on screen, then turned to negative colours as a synthesizer droned a minor chord. Most of the show had been interviews with one of the detectives who worked on his sister's case, and who made it very clear that he thought Dykma had gotten away with it. Dykma had died a few years before and couldn't defend himself.

Becky said, "Your mom was so mad about it. They interviewed her for five hours. She opened up to them. Told them stories about Laura. And they only used maybe thirty seconds of it. I remember she called me the night it aired in tears. She couldn't believe it. I thought she would have told you."

"I guess it didn't come up."

"Your mom always said how you didn't like to talk about your sister." David stared at her. "I told your mom I would honour her wishes and not talk to any media again. But then, a few months ago, James sent me a message over Facebook. He had such a different approach. He is from here, you know—"

"He mentioned that."

"—and he has a real, genuine urge to tell this story. He knew, right away, all the problems with the *Murder in a Small Town* thing. He could tell we'd all been misrepresented. So, we got talking, and James sent me a list of errors in the documentary. Factual things. A lot of it was silly stuff, like they kept using a shot of Mount McAllister when they should have been using your mountain. They got the name of the hospital here wrong. James told me those errors made him think they had to have gotten a lot more wrong. So he looked into it. And he found out some things. Some things that you might want to hear."

"Like what?"

"It's not my place to say."

"I'm not going to talk to him, so you might as well tell me."

"I really should let James tell you." David waited. She said, "James doesn't think that Greg Dykma is responsible for killing Laura."

David said, "That's it?"

"What do you mean 'That's it?'"

"No one but my parents and the cops thought that."

"You didn't?"

"He was our neighbour for, like, five years before that happened. Why would he just decide one day to kill someone?"

"That's exactly what your mom said. You thought she thought he did?"

"Why else would she be in that documentary?"

"She didn't know they were going to make the whole thing about Dykma. That's why she was so mad. They made it look like she agreed with them."

They both adjusted to the new information.

"Your salad, and you've got the burger." Sue put the plates down and asked Becky if she needed anything else. After she left, David got up and grabbed the malt vinegar from the front counter. He slid back into the booth and covered his fries with it. Becky scrunched up her nose and he added some more.

He said, "Anyways, I'm still not interested. Every

few years these guys show up and want to write something about Laura and it's always exactly the same, but maybe they say Dykma did it or, like, the four-by-four club knew something about it, like that podcast a couple years ago. Your guy can cut and paste the article from last time and spin a wheel to find a new suspect."

"He doesn't want it to be like that. He's really concerned with the town. With the people. He wants to write about Laura. He felt like she was always secondary in stories about her. That her death has been sensationalized, taken away from the people who were affected by it. From us." She reached across the table and put her hands on David's.

"That's literally what they always say. Like, word for word I have received the same message every time. I'm surprised my mom got tricked again."

"No, I swear. He was very clear, from the beginning, he didn't want to do it without family involvement. He was so sincere that after I spoke with him a couple of times, I went to your mom on his behalf. They spoke, and she thought he was just as sincere as I did. Your mom found the interviews with him to be cathartic" — David was sure that was a word his mom wouldn't have used — "and she had opened up to him. She knew he would respect the story, and our memories, and Laura."

David popped a fry in his mouth. He said, "Not interested."

Becky closed her eyes and drew in a deep breath. David took a bite out of his burger. She opened her eyes and said, "I understand it's difficult for you. Your mom always told me how much you didn't like to talk about Laura. I want to respect your boundaries. But your mom left a few things unsaid that James was hoping to talk to you about. And she had a box of papers about Laura she wanted to give him."

"I haven't seen anything like that."

"It was," she said, "what your mom wanted. I think you should honour her last wish."

David pushed himself out of the booth and said, "Pleasure as always, Becky." He pulled out his jacket and headed to the door, then turned around and went back. Becky looked at him hopefully. He picked up his plate. At the counter, he asked Sue for a to-go box.

"Breaking hearts?" Sue asked.

"A friend of my sister's, Sue."

"Oh," she said. "Shit. That reminds me. Some guy came in here yesterday asking about her for some article or something."

"You're fucking kidding me."

"I figured you wouldn't want anyone talking about it, so I told him to fuck off."

"Sue, you're the best." David picked up the box and left a twenty on the counter. "That's just for me. And thank you."

CHAPTER SEVEN

GRIFFITHS WAS JUST CLOSE enough to Victoria, and the houses were just that much cheaper, that it had become a commuter town a decade before. The drive was an hour, but people who liked nature and space could justify the time. There was the river, hiking, the ocean. It was pretty. The population had doubled, but the infrastructure hadn't kept up. The four-lane highway through town had a dozen traffic lights; it could take forty-five minutes to get from one end to the other in the afternoon. David took the back roads home to avoid traffic.

The road followed the river up to the old hospital and the town's first suburb, small bungalows with large yards built in the fifties, then the new suburbs from

the eighties that were now "the bad part of town" —
rundown townhouse complexes, what had once been
a video store and now sold vapes, the curling rink,
a bar. After Frenchman's Corners, which was not a
proper corner anymore but instead a roundabout that
David's mom had complained about every day — "No
one knows how to use these stupid roundabouts," she'd
say, meaning she didn't know how to use them and
always nearly hit someone — David had to brake at a
line of cars.

He waited. Rolled a few car lengths. Thought about
turning off and trying his luck with the highway, but
then the cars moved forward a dozen metres before
stopping. He waited again, then rolled ahead and
stopped beside his telephone pole.

David had hit the pole the year after he graduated.
He'd misjudged the curve of the road while driving
home drunk and drifted into the wrong lane, over-
compensated to get back on the right side of the road,
and fishtailed around the corner. The back end of his
station wagon hit the pole, and the car spun around
and rolled down the embankment, landing on its roof.
David crawled out of the car. He didn't seem too hurt,
so he grabbed his CDs out of the glove compartment
and removed the anti-theft faceplate from the player
and walked home. The police showed up the next morning. His mom's frantic yelling woke David up — he

still lived in his old room then. He came down, hung-over and sore all over. It took him a minute to realize what was going on.

The police had no way to prove he'd been drunk — when the cop asked David, he said, "How could I get a drink, I'm eighteen?" — so he just got a ticket for leaving the scene of an accident, which he successfully fought. This was before cellphones; there was no way to call for help and the judge believed David when he said that since no one was hurt, he thought he could wait until morning to deal with it.

David learned later, when insurance sent a bill, that when you hit a telephone pole and are at fault, you have to pay to replace it. David didn't have any money, so his dad paid it and David paid him back three hundred dollars a month for the next eighteen months. His dad never spoke to him about the accident after the debt was paid, but forced the phrase "your telephone pole" into conversation whenever he could: "Oh, just turn left past your telephone pole." "They're putting in a new subdivision right by your telephone pole."

His dad had refused to loan David money for a new car, and he couldn't get the bank to help because he was on EI after his first summer at the golf course, so he didn't get another car until the par-three opened in the spring. He spent that winter walking from home into town and back again at night if he couldn't get a ride. It was a distance that had seemed impossible to walk growing up, but it only took an hour. It was a long hour, though, walking by the same things he'd driven by his whole life.

The line of cars moved forward. When they stopped again, David saw a cop walking down the yellow line in the middle of the road. He said a few words at each car and then moved on. One car did a U-turn after he passed by. The rest moved forward to fill the space.

David rolled down his window. The cop came up to it and leaned in. "Sorry for the delay."

"What's going on?"

"It's a police matter."

"Any idea how long?"

"Wouldn't want to guess."

The cop looked ready to move on, but David managed to say, "I live on Mountain Road, just wondering if I should turn around and go to the highway."

The cop said, "Oh, shit. You're almost there." Speaking to a local homeowner, he turned friendly. "We're just wrapping up. It'll be a couple minutes."

"Thanks."

"Yeah, we got a tip that guy who beat that whore out by Bradey's Lake Road was hiding out in one of the old farmhouses on Robertson. A buddy of that Sanderson guy owns land up there and someone thought he was holed up in a barn. We were ready for him to come shooting his way out. We got our tactical unit in and everything. But he wasn't there. Nothing but cow and chicken shit."

"I'm glad you didn't have to shoot anyone."

"Would save us a lot of fucking time if we could have. The whole thing was a waste of time. Hooker steals drugs, hooker gets beat up. Who gives a fuck? Let them all kill each other, I say. Saves me walking a hundred fucking miles in the sun." He laughed.

David said, "Ha."

"Anyways, you sit tight, we'll be done in a minute."

The cars started to move soon after. At the Robertson turnoff, David saw a line of police cars and what Jamie had been right to call a tank. Two police officers stood in front of it with assault rifles across their chests, another held a cellphone up, taking pictures.

The road curved and entered the last bit of farmland in the area. This was the only stretch of road that was unchanged from when David was young. A barn with a collapsing roof. Cows that had to be new but looked the same as always. The double bump of the mountain came into view around the curve of the road. He drove toward it.

Growing up, there had only been the four houses in their neighbourhood: theirs, the Murrays', and the one belonging to an old German couple who lived at the end of the street. When they were young, David and Laura had played with their grandchildren's Power Wheels. A fourth house, on the corner of Sherman Road and the old highway, was the old Sherman farm. It had been John Sherman, the great-grandson of the pioneer settler who had built the farm, who sold the non-arable back half of the farm to a developer to pay debts that had been plaguing the family since the start of the Second World War. The development had stalled after David's parents moved in, and the neighbourhood was unchanged for his childhood, up until the gravel pit went in.

A few years after Laura died, the gravel pit sold to a different developer, and with the other suburbs of town grown out closer to their house, development began. The pit became "The Mountainside," which had grown around David's house and now stretched up two-thirds of the mountain. The town had been worried that the whole mountain would be taken over by development, but the developer got permission to build the final phase by promising to turn the top of the mountain into a park. They had put in hiking trails and a BMX park. There was a new lookout on top of the mountain which David had never been to.

The Mountainside had led to the area all around David's house getting developed. The Murray house was gone, torn down after they moved and replaced with three houses. The only thing left of them was the boulder with their address on it, now with two more added. The old German man had died a few months before Laura — he'd been sick for a long time, lost a leg to diabetes, and was on oxygen. The widow sold. Their house was still there, but now surrounded by others. David's house was surrounded by others too. The development his dad had thought he was buying into came, just a few decades late. He had died as ground was broken on the Mountainside.

Aside from David's house, the last twenty acres of the Sherman farm was the only thing the same as it always had been. Houses now crowded the field. The new people complained about the smell of cows and chickens and the noise of the tractor. There wasn't anything to be done about it; the farm had been there since the city was founded. Everyone was waiting for John III to sell off the land when his dad died.

Mr. Sherman, the fifth Sherman since the town's founding, was on his tractor spreading manure when David drove by, not looking particularly close to death. He recognized the car and stretched himself upright to wave. David tapped the horn as he drove by. The double bump of the mountain shifted, the closer one became more prominent, and then David was in the early dusk of the mountain.

A note had been tucked into the side door, between the door and the frame, from James.

CHAPTER EIGHT

DAVID'S DAD BOUGHT A Tandy 1000 in 1986. Personal computers were new and the idea of a computer room hadn't taken hold, so the computer went in the living room, like a second TV, on a little desk in an alcove that had previously held a china hutch. It stayed there through high school, when David's mom and dad felt they needed to monitor the time he spent on his 386. Only after David moved into the basement did the computer move out of the living room. It was put in his old bedroom, which his dad turned into an office. That didn't last. His mom liked to watch TV while she played her games, so the computer set-up moved back down.

David pulled out his mom's computer chair and tossed her little flattened pillow on the couch. He jiggled the mouse; his mom never turned off her computer. The computer hummed into action slowly. McAfee let him know the computer was in danger. Internet Explorer wanted to update. The printer was "Ready." David cleared the pop-ups, which were replaced with more. He had bought her this computer right after his dad died, to replace the Pentium that was well past the end of its life. He'd tried to get her a new one a few years earlier, but she refused. "Every time you fiddle with my computer I can't find anything ever again," she'd said. He waited for the processor to catch up with the clicks.

Her landing page was Yahoo. The typeface was large. He scrolled down her bookmark tab, which was open along the side of the browser. There were, it seemed, thousands of bookmarked pages. She had somehow managed to figure out how to have icons for her most visited sites along the top of the browser. News, email, Facebook, Candy Crush. He clicked email.

She had 256 unread messages, most notifications from Facebook letting her know someone had commented or tagged her. David deleted all those and was left with a dozen unread messages. Seven were automatically sent bills or notifications. Two were from friends in the days before the obituary went out. Three were from James Moore. Two of the subject lines were "Can't get in touch?" The oldest, from the day after she died, was "Recordings and Trip West."

James wrote that he was coming to town, looked to confirm dates, and closed with "I attached the recordings of our interviews so far. Like I said when you asked for them, I wouldn't normally send these to an interviewee, so I do need to reiterate: I can't change anything I write about at the request of an interviewee. Thanks, as always, for trusting me to tell this story. I know it's difficult for you. — James." There were three audio files attached.

David searched for more emails from James. There were a dozen and they didn't tell him much. The first outlined what Becky had told David: James making a case for his sincerity. David's mom had replied in her way — unfinished sentences strung together with ellipses. "I had a bad experience . . . I don't know if I can talk about Laura . . . you seem nice and Becky did mention you'd be in touch . . . I need to think about it." He responded saying he understood, of course, her reluctance, and he would not pester her. He wrote that he always tried to put family first in these situations and to humanize people. He said she could read some of his work. David opened the link. It went to the website of a glossy magazine David had seen on the newspaper racks but never bought. A banner at the top of the article said, "Winner of the National Magazine Award."

The story was about a rich couple in Toronto who had been murdered. David remembered the case. It had been big news at the time. The couple were killed by their son, who had used a speargun. A bomb squad had been dispatched to the son's condo after the bodies had been discovered, closing several blocks of downtown Toronto. There hadn't been a bomb, but that the son used a speargun made the story memorable, it being an unusual weapon for a parricide.

James's article, published a year after the murder, filled in the unknown parts of the story. The bomb squad had been called in because the police had found an elaborate series of electronic and analog contraptions in the son's apartment. James, through interviews and crime scene photos, reconstructed what had been a failed plan: At 2 p.m., an old bell-style alarm clock was set to go off. That would cause a pencil with an aluminum finger stylus on the end to fall onto the son's cellphone, sending a text message to a friend. A second, similar device, rigged to three bobbing birds, was set up over his keyboard — they would post a Facebook message, switch tabs, and then post a private message to his girlfriend, several minutes apart, starting at 2:15 p.m. Security cameras had caught him leaving the apartment in an elaborate disguise. He'd bought a speargun with a prepaid credit card, purchased with bitcoin, and hidden it in his parents' garage a week before. He might have got away with it, but his mom screamed when the spear hit her. His dad came out before he could get the second shot ready — the speargun was more difficult to reload than he'd thought — so he'd been forced to stab his dad with the spear. The ensuing fight had taken them out of the house. A neighbour called 911. The father died before the police showed up, the son too exhausted from the fight to run.

James wrote about the kid's past. He had been top of his class in private school but got caught cheating in college. His parents smoothed that over and he graduated, though not with honours. He tried several businesses after school, all of which failed, and then he tried to rob a bank. The record of this had been so well buried by the parents that James was the first person to discover it. The kid had developed another complicated plan: a recorded message on a loudspeaker drew the police to a bank on one side of town while he went into another and robbed it the old-fashioned way — with a Nixon mask and a fake gun. The fake gun had not fooled the security guard, who punched the kid on his way out. He had been charged but served no time, and his criminal record was expunged — this was the work of the wealthy parents. After, he went back to failing at almost-legitimate business. He tried to put on a music festival that came to nothing and put him in debt his parents bailed him out of. He became a cryptocurrency investment consultant and lost people hundreds of thousands of dollars. His parents couldn't bail him out of that one, which is what led him to one last plan: murdering his parents to get his inheritance.

James closed with a quote from an uncle. "There was nothing they wouldn't have done for him. No parents loved their child more. And that's what got them killed, because he just couldn't see that." It was a good read. David could see why it had won an award.

David searched for more stories by James, but only turned up profiles of new businesses in Toronto that he had written and a weekly column about renovation budgets. James's LinkedIn showed he'd been a staff writer and editor for something called AroundTO, where those articles had appeared, before going freelance a year earlier.

David went back to the emails. His mom had written James back a few days after the first exchange, asking for him to call to talk it over. There wasn't anything else of interest—quick questions from James and confirming the times for calls—David's mom preferred to talk on the phone.

David opened the email with the recordings and downloaded the audio files. Each was dated. They were from February 12, 19, and March 8—the last, he realized, the night she died. He clicked the oldest one.

Nothing happened. He clicked it again and his mom's computer froze. He was about to restart it when the computer, from somewhere deep in its processor, lurched into action enough to open Winamp. David hit Play. While he waited for the computer to start playing the file, he turned on his mom's speaker. Eventually, a man's voice said, "... okay, this is recording."

James was sorry he had to have her on speaker-phone, but it was the only way to get both of their voices. Because of privacy laws, he said, it was sur-prisingly difficult to get an app that recorded phone conversations. He sounded uncertain, nervous.

David's mom said, "I can hear you just fine."

She would have been sitting on her chair with the TV muted, shifting the portable from ear to ear as her neck got tired of holding it place. David would have heard these conversations as low murmurs though the floor; she would often talk to friends on the phone for hours.

She said she was surprised to be talking to a repor-ter, actually. "Those documentary people treated me so badly a few years back. But we've talked all about that," she said. "Anyways, you must have your questions."

James thought the documentary was a good place to start, actually. He said, "We've talked about what they got wrong and how I want to correct that. Would you mind, I guess, talking about that. You never thought it was Greg Dykma?"

"Of course not. Why on earth would he do some-thing like that to someone he'd lived next to for years?

I told that to those stupid documentary people and they went with what that detective said anyways. It's just so frustrating." His mom was agitated. David knew she would have been sitting, leaning forward out of her armchair. Gesturing with her free hand. "They make a mistake early on and then just keep making it worse. You know, they ruined that poor man's life."

"How do you mean?"

"The police just needed someone to investigate, so it looked like they were doing something, and he was all they had. I want you to print that. You write that the police did nothing at all the first two days. They kept telling us it was normal for girls to run away and they would keep an eye out for her and all that, but they didn't look. They barely checked where she ran. They didn't check the logging roads. If that truck driver hadn't found her music player way back on the logging roads, who knows how long it would have been before anyone looked on the mountain."

"Did you tell the police you thought they were on the wrong track?"

"They don't care what the family thinks unless the family agrees with them. And that was the problem. Once they had to actually do some work, they picked the easiest person. And they came in here and asked about him and Harold, and Harold wanted someone to blame as much as the cops. So, once they start down that road it's hard to bring them back. Men are prideful, you know. They don't like to be wrong." She paused a moment, then said, "I should say it's men of my generation. I see it in the younger boys a little less. With some of them, I mean. Men will always be men."

James asked, "Why did your husband not like Greg Dykma?"

Silence, while his mom considered.

"Well, he would have said it was because Dykma was a . . . excuse the word—a skid. You know. Drank and smoked grass and lived in a trailer and all that. But him not liking Greg Dykma had more to do, I think, with pride, again. His own pride. You know, Harold always hated living out here."

"Why was that?"

"He had wanted a certain type of home. His dad emigrated to Canada and they were all raised poor— the eight kids all out on the farm in Saskatchewan. The older brothers moved out as soon as they could to get away. Harold was still in elementary school, and he heard about all the great things they were doing out in the world while he was stuck at home. They'd visit and have these fancy cars and show pictures of their big houses and have these wives. But it was all a show, his brothers. They were . . . well, one of his older brothers drank himself to death before he turned forty. The other actually made some money, but he lost it all to divorces and new women. He asked me for a loan, if you can believe it, at Harold's funeral. He lives in a trailer now in Swift Current now. I don't have anything to do with him.

"Harold never saw his brothers like that though. You can never really get past the, what's it called, hero worship you have when you're a kid for an older brother. He thought they had it made. So when he was sixteen he went out, got away from his family, to find success like those brothers. He chased work in construction and made good money doing that, but after he got out here and we got together and had a kid, he needed something more reliable. We couldn't be following work out to Alberta or wherever with kids. So he quit construction and got a job out at the truss plant. He still had these big plans, but he changed them to fit in with family life. He figured he'd work there, learn how to do it, and take over. He got this house as a starter home then. It was supposed to be a big development, which it is now, but that took years. It was something about the septic fields and not being able to run a sewage pipe out here. Anyways, the first twenty-five years we were here, only three places were built.

"And then, the old man never sold the company and he lived a long time. The kids, who hadn't cared about the company when they were young, got older and saw it as a stable source of income, which it was. When the old man died, they got the company. Harold was furious. This was in the early 2000s. He thought he had a verbal agreement with the dad, but the will had been clear—everything went to the kids. So, he got arguing with these boys all the time. He thought they didn't know anything, and really they didn't. The place is out of business now and it's because the kids didn't know how to treat the regulars right. But he could have been a bit more . . . diplomatic is the word. Anyways, he was given notice and a buyout. He was still young enough to work then but he was just furious. Couldn't let it go. And then he died. His heart, you know. And I always thought it was because he got so worked up about things. I mean, he smoked for years and didn't eat very well. That doesn't help either.

"But I was saying, before all the stuff with work, that this neighbourhood didn't become what he wanted. He never liked it out here—he thought it was like where he grew up, some little house in the middle of nowhere—and it had devalued so quick, he didn't want to sell it at a loss. He was so stubborn and prideful—please don't print that, he was a good man, but you know, men can be like that. He always felt like he'd been had and it made him upset. It was almost like he couldn't see what we had because it wasn't what he thought he wanted.

"His problem with the gravel pit came from all that. It was the last straw for him. He thought it was killing

the last of his property value. That he went from living in the middle of nowhere to living in the middle of
nowhere with an industrial plant and trucks rumbling
by. And Greg Dykma moved onto the lot and kind of
became...I don't know. All the anger focused on him,
even before Laura died. He was a...what's that word?"

"A scapegoat?"

"That's right. And it wasn't fair."

THEY'D FOUND OUT ABOUT the gravel pit on a Monday
morning when David was in grade seven and Laura in
grade eight. The family was eating breakfast. Outside,
air brakes hissed and everyone looked out the living
room window. A flatbed semi truck couldn't make the
corner from Sherman onto Mountain. The truck was
on the thin strip of grass on the far side of the ditch,
the trailer stuck out down Sherman at a sharp angle.
They could see the driver, craning his neck around and
spinning the wheel.

Harold said, "What is that truck doing on our lawn."

David asked, "Is that our lawn?"

"Don't be smart," his dad said. David had become lit-
eral in a way his dad hated; the lawn was technically city
land. Harold let it go when the air brakes popped again
and the truck tires pivoted, digging themselves deeper
into the shoulder. Harold put on his shoes and went out.

David watched him cross the lawn. Mr. Murray, from across Sherman, showed up at the same time. The driver of the truck opened the door and got down to the running board. They spoke, gestured. The driver got back in and the two men directed the truck around the corner; it lurched, the air brakes hissed. Then David's dad came in and said, "They're putting in a gravel pit."

David's dad spent the next week calling people and trying to figure out "Why the hell they were allowed to put an industrial gravel pit in a quiet, residential neighbourhood?" The answer turned out to be surprisingly complicated.

In the 1860s, a surveyor had divided the land in the valley into equal plots for the government to distribute to anyone willing to immigrate. The land was given away by lottery, sight unseen. Some people moved into good farmland around the river and lakes — those families became the ones that had their names on the schools and roads all over town. Those who got undesirable land didn't do so well. The family that got the homestead land that would become the gravel pit moved to the valley that would eventually be named Griffiths to find their property was mostly vertical rock. The one small, flat patch of arable land was in the shadow of the mountain and only got a few hours of sunlight every day. They stuck it out a few years and then left for the gold rush and never returned. A great-great-grandson who had lived his whole life in Arkansas was surprised to learn that he was entitled to a piece of land in Canada and that someone wanted to buy it. A development company based in Guelph, Ontario, had contacted him. They specialized in going through town archives to find unclaimed, forgotten land, and then connected local developers with the owners in exchange for a small cut of the deal.

A clerk at city hall explained the history of the property to Harold, and then, at his request, a city councillor called to explain why the zoning had been allowed to change from agricultural to industrial. This was before dinner a week after the first truck had gone by. Harold took the call at the dinner table. The family watched him, listening. Harold said, "Now hold on — " His face turned red while he listened more, then he said again, "Now hold on, what sort of public consultation? We're the only 'public' on this road." And then, "A sign? On a dead-end road!?" He put his hand over the mouthpiece and asked if anyone had seen a "proposal to zoning change" sign on the property.

David had walked by it every time he'd gone up the mountain for the past six months. It was halfway up Mountain Road on his way to the logging road gate. David said, "No."

When no one at city hall cared that he was a taxpayer and homeowner whose property value was being affected by this, Harold changed his approach. He called bylaw officers. By then, blasting at the gravel pit had begun, and periodically throughout the day the house would rattle. The first few times, David's mom had come running into the living room and yelled for the kids to get under the table while she stood in the door frame, terrified.

That complaint got Harold nowhere; the company had done their due diligence with permits. Harold tried to argue pollution. He claimed the safety of his kids. He wrote a letter to the editor that appeared in the local paper, and sent a clipping of it to the city. He went before council with a list of infractions. By then, the pit was already dug. During the day, the low rumble of the grater never stopped; it was too late to stop a project in process, even if they'd wanted to. Harold did manage to get the company fined — the fish-bearing creek that ran through the Shermans' had completely dried up. The fine was paid, but the creek never ran again.

Another concession from the company was that they had to pave Mountain Road, between Sherman and the gate to the logging road, and have street lamps put in. "Civic improvements through private capital" — David's dad read the quoted city councillor in the paper to them; he slammed the paper down and said, "It's a fucking dead end."

After the regular blasting stopped, they got used to the gravel pit. Gravel trucks went by a few times a day. It was no worse than the logging trucks coming in and out in the spring. Since the road was paved, David no longer had to wash the dust off his dad's car every weekend. And Laura could use it to train on. Before, she'd have to stay late after school or get a ride in the evening to get to the track. Now, with a paved and lit road, she could just run right out her door. Their dad complained about the lost house value, the trucks, the danger, but everyone got used to it.

And then, the summer before David started grade eleven, Greg Dykma moved in. They found out about it in the morning. They were, again, all at the breakfast table. Harold looked out the window and said, "Whose dog is that?"

A large dog strained to take a shit on their lawn. Someone said, loud enough to be heard through the closed window, "Baby, get over here, you bitch," and then Dykma jumped over the ditch and pulled the dog across the lawn. Another dog trotted into view and rammed its nose into the first's butt.

Harold went down to the front door. Greg crossed the lawn toward him. The dogs bit and snapped at each other, but followed. Greg waved at David and Laura in the window.

Harold waited for Greg to come to him and then said, "Can I help you?"

"Just letting the dogs get to know the neighbour-hood. This is Baby and Killer. Just names. Rotties get a bad rep, but they're gentle bitches." He slapped one dog's haunch. It flopped on the ground and wagged its tail.

"You moved in . . . ?"

"I'm the new security at the gravel pit. Greg Dykma." He held out his hand.

Harold said, "You live there?"

At dinner that night, their dad told them the city clerk had told him that, though the pit was not zoned for residential use, they were allowed to have on-site security, who could live in a non-permanent structure. Harold said he couldn't believe that not only did they add an industrial park to a residential area, but now he also had to deal with a "trailer-trash skid decreasing his property value."

He couldn't force him out, so he went back to bylaws. The only complaint that got anywhere was about the dogs — Dykma started to keep them on leashes off the property and he never tried to speak to Harold again.

"A FEW DAYS AFTER they knew Laura was on the mountain somewhere," Barbara said to James, on the recording, "the police started asking questions that were... well, we realized they were asking about Dykma very quickly. And Harold... I don't know. He jumped on it. He thought, of course it had to be him, because he hated Dykma and needed to blame someone. And he was so sure. He was so sure he was right and wouldn't listen to anyone about it. I couldn't even bring it up. And the police were sure they were right too. They kept bringing him in for questioning and they never found any way to tie it to him because there wasn't. But that one detective would not let it go — that's the one from that documentary I went on. And the poor man had to clear out of town because everyone thought he had done it, and it was all because of this... this pride, I think. Like I said, they screwed up early on but never would admit that. They had to have a suspect.

"But the thing that happened, to Harold, was he started to blame himself, I think. He thought that if he'd fought harder, the pit would never have gone in, and if the pit hadn't gone in, Laura wouldn't have run along the road. He just... he felt like his job was to protect his children and he failed to do that. And God knows I thought that way myself. You know, 'What did I do wrong, how could I have prevented it?' But there's only so much you can control, you know? Harold couldn't see it had nothing to do with him at all. Men have trouble with that, you know. That they're not the most important person in every story. He never saw that, and never forgave himself."

CHAPTER NINE

DAVID PAUSED THE RECORDING and a pop-up warned him that the computer needed updating. He clicked "update later" and the computer froze. He waited. Clicked. Hit Enter. Then CTRL-ALT-DLT. Nothing happened. He watched the blank screen for a minute and then a dialogue box popped up with a "COMPUTER UPDATING, DO NOT RESTART" message. David watched the progress bar stop at 3 percent. The grinding noise started.

He took the cordless phone out of the drawer and checked that the battery was still removed. He looked along the walls for a forgotten phone jack and then opened drawers and cupboards. He pulled out plates, bowls, cups — all mismatched sets from years of replacing things as they broke. He looked at the mess he'd made while he waited for the noise to start again. It did not.

He went out to the car and came back with a pile of flat boxes. He sorted out the four best plates and put the rest in a box. He did the same with the cups and the bowls and then emptied the rest of the cupboards. Rusted baking sheets, mismatched pots and pans, an iron griddle and a George Foreman Grill, jugs and pitchers, apple corer, Slap Chop. All the accumulated kitchen stuff that his mom didn't need but couldn't throw out because it was "still good."

The food in the pantry he hadn't been able to turn into meals went into another box — old bags of flour, boxes of herbal teas, dried beans he didn't know how to prepare. In the bottom kitchen cabinets, among the non-stick pans made toxic by scraped bottoms, pots, cookie jars, and rolls of tin foil, he found an old rotary phone, wrapped up in cables. Before the house had a portable, they'd bought extra-long cables so they could take the phone out of the living room. The cord wound up into a plastic box. David put the phone on the counter, beside the disconnected cordless.

He wrote DONATION on the side of the boxes and stacked them by the side door. The grinding started while he was putting down a box of large wooden salad bowls and plastic pitchers. It had stopped by the time he got back to the kitchen.

David had once read an article about a beeping noise that had haunted a man for years. He had complained about it on Reddit and the internet got invested in helping solve the mystery. Pictures of the house were taken. Advice offered. The owner disconnected the main power of his house for three days and still heard the noise, at unpredictable intervals, all hours of the day. He set up microphones, but the noise was too faint to pick up. Eventually, a noise-sourcing specialist had flown across the country and moved in for a week on his own dime. He had special mics and expertise, but turned up, again, nothing. The man had been ready to sell the house when he accidentally came across what was causing it: an old digital watch in a drawer. It looked dead—the screen was not lit up—but it would beep sometimes to indicate its battery needed changing. The owner had seen the watch many times on his searches, but with no power, he never thought that the noise was coming from it.

It took three tries for David to open the drawer his mom kept random things in—a single metal chopstick had gotten stuck, preventing it from opening. On top, a pack of cards, an oven mitt, a rubber ball, and a stapler. He pulled the drawer right out and dumped everything on the kitchen table. A child's bouncy ball rolled off the edge and bounced along the kitchen floor and under the fridge. There were a pair of scissors, a hole punch, candles, matches, screwdrivers. Also, empty matchboxes, crumpled paper, an exploded bag of drink umbrellas, loose change, half a pair of scissors. David did find a watch — his dad's Rolex, which he had been accused of flushing down the toilet when he was a toddler and that his mom found behind their bedroom armoire after Harold died — but it was a wind-up, not electric, and had no alarm besides.

The grinding started. With nothing in the kitchen to absorb or deflect it, the sound seemed to be coming from the cupboard by the fridge. David reached up and put his hand on a bare shelf, felt vibration with the noise. By the time he got a chair to stand on, the noise had stopped. He craned his head up above the cupboard.

When the house was built, a vent had been installed to help heat passively rise to the upstairs bedrooms. It had never really worked — they always used baseboard heaters in their rooms — but when he and Laura were young and their mom needed to get them downstairs or let them know there was a phone call, she would go into the kitchen and shout up through the vent. Other times, Laura and David would lie by it at night, stretched out across the hall with one foot in their rooms, so they could claim they were in their rooms if caught, and listen to conversations when their parents had people over. When the kitchen had been remodelled after David moved into the basement, the new cabinets went almost to the ceiling, hiding the vent.

The noise started again, the grinding loud enough that David jumped back and then had to catch himself on a shelf in the open cupboard, which came loose from its bracket. He managed to get a foot under him as he fell off the chair. He leaned the shelf against the fridge.

David walked to the bottom of the stairs and then up. The top floor of the house was just a hall with four doors. The wheel marks left by the stretcher led straight down the hall and into his parents' room. On the right, his old room, and the upstairs bathroom. On the left, Laura's room. The vent stuck out from under her door. Someone had not lined up the plans right, and the thin wall had been built over the vent, bisecting it so that a quarter was in Laura's room. He went in.

Laura's room hadn't changed since he was young. Pink ballerina wallpaper that had been put up when Laura was eight and danced had faded, covered with collages of photos—she'd gone once each weekend to the one-hour photo place in the town mall—of Becky, Robyn, sport events, fundraisers, school dances. Her books, a neat stack of *YM* magazines, *Tiger Beat*, *Teen Vogue*, from when she was younger, and the ones she actually read—*Cosmo*, *Vogue*—underneath those. Board games stacked along a shelf: Girl Talk, which she never let David play, Candyland from when she was young—she'd always held onto things, been nostalgic for years just past. Books, poetry, Dickinson, but also a strange amount of mysticism—books about gems, the Enneagram, dream interpretation. And a large book of medical problems and home remedies. Her bed still had the quilt their great-grandma had made for her. Lots of pillows. It was tightly tucked in and smelled faintly of fabric softener. David had always figured his mom had left it, but it was a surprise that she would come in, vacuum, dust, and clean, and then put everything back in its place.

The only thing different in the room was a large box on Laura's writing desk. On the side and lid, David's mom had written in Sharpie: LAURA BOX and DOCUMENTS. He looked inside, the box was filled to the top with folders.

David opened the blinds. They were stiff.

He hadn't seen the front yard from this angle in twenty years. The memory of the view didn't agree with what he saw. The trees were bigger. The hedge that had marked the edge of their property and now blocked the neighbours' house from view had grown into a line of trees. They were no longer trimmed; they just grew out. The little cherry tree had become a big cherry tree. The apple tree was gone. There was a house across the street now, and another next door, visible between the overgrown trees. Everything was dark in the shadow of the mountain's early dusk.

The noise started again, loud, behind him. On a small table by the door there was a phone. It was an eighties novelty, a see-though model. Laura won it for selling the most Christmas wrapping paper for a school fundraiser in grade six. When it worked, gears spun and lights blinked. The lights were dead. But the oversized red and purple gears still tried to spin and the ringer made a feeble, electronic whir. The vibration ran down the side table leg, which was on the vent. It had probably been ringing that like that since Laura died, the gears slowly breaking down, the light burning out. The noise a little below what either of his parents could hear.

The gears stopped. David turned back to the window. James Moore's car had parked on the shoulder of the road. David ducked down.

He thought about crawling to the switch to turn off the light, but that would draw attention to the fact that it had been on. The downstairs lights were on anyways. And it was dusk and he had been lit from behind. He knew he had probably been seen. But he stayed down. Waited through the ringing doorbell and watched Laura's phone try to work. Five minutes after his sister's phone lurched into motion for the third time, he peeked over the edge of the windowsill. The car had left. He picked up the box and went downstairs.

CHAPTER TEN

DAVID CARTED A DONATION box into Thrift Town. The guy inside had worked there since David was in high school and would go in to go through records or search for gas station jackets or bowling shirts. He told David he could leave the donations by the door. There was a large pile of boxes there already, their sides collapsed and leaning. David tried to put one on top, then just stacked it in front. By the time he had brought in all of them, the aisle was blocked. David thought he should ask if that was okay. He waited by the till, then walked to the back of the store. He couldn't find the guy anywhere. David flipped through the records for a minute but there was nothing — Zamfir, classical, Nana Mouskouri. He didn't have the patience for digging anymore. The guy was still not at the counter. A woman stepped over the pile. David shrugged and said sorry. She smiled. She looked familiar, but so did everyone in town. David decided to leave. The woman followed him out the door. They went to their cars.

He stretched his back by his mom's SUV. The high school was kitty-corner to where he'd parked, across the highway. A large sign advertising school events faced the road. It said, PROM TICKETS NOW AVAILABLE. GAME FRIDAY. GO TURDS. The school team was called the Thunderbirds and abbreviated T-birds, which made changing the sign easy; it was a gag that went back to when his mom was a student. He made eye contact with the woman, who had also been looking at the sign. She smiled at him and said, "Go you turds."

The voice did it. He said, "Holy shit, Carolyn Murray. From across Sherman?"

And she said, "Oh my God, David."

Three days after his sister's funeral, a "for sale" sign appeared on the Murray's front yard, and later that day a moving truck came and loaded all their things. His mom brought it up sometimes— "And the Murrays just left," she would say. "They never even called. We were neighbours for fifteen years."

David said, "You don't live here, do you?"

"In Nanaimo. I just had a meeting and decided to walk around a bit after. I thought you looked familiar in the store, but it's been so long I couldn't place it." She laughed. It was warm and infectious and dispelled the awkwardness he normally would have felt around an old friend of his sister's. He laughed too.

"Were you meeting with that reporter?"

"What reporter?"

"Never mind."

She said, "It doesn't look like you're doing much. Grab a coffee with me?"

They left their cars and walked. At the corner of the highway, waiting for the light to change, Carolyn broke the silence that had started to drag by saying, "How are the fighting Turds doing this year?" They both laughed again. She said, "What about you? You're still here?"

"I am."

She picked up his tone. "Oh no. You're not still at the same house?"

"I am," he said, a bit more definitively. "But I moved into the basement — it's not like I'm in the same room. There has been progress. Downward progress, but progress." He told her a short version of the last twenty years while they walked. His job, how it never really made sense to move out, and how he fixed up the basement — "It's pretty nice down there," he lied — and he told her his dad died years before, which she had heard, and that his mom had just died, which she hadn't and was sorry about.

He said, "It's okay, she was old."

"You haven't changed much."

They went to Café de la Lune, up the street, between the high school and the park where high-school kids smoked pot. As long as one person in your group bought a coffee, you could sit on the patio as long as you wanted. Kids who looked like the kids he would have hung out with hung out in front.

David and Carolyn stood in line. The owner was the same. He put his hand on the small of a barista's back and said "behind you." He corrected the angle of another barista's coffee pour.

They went outside and he looked up at the sky and said, "That sounds really low."

There was a helicopter somewhere south of them. It sounded like it was below the treeline, where the canyon opened up and the river flattened out and slowed down as it entered town.

Carolyn said, "I wonder what that's all about?"

"They've been looking for a guy who beat up a hooker. Probably something to do with that."

Carolyn said, "Sex worker."

"What?"

"Sorry. I just mean 'hooker' is not the word to use anymore. Sex worker is less harsh."

"Sorry, I didn't..."

"My dad still says hooker even though I've been at

him for years. I try to correct people because it comes up a lot in my work. Don't worry about it."

They walked in silence for a minute before David said, "So you're a sex worker these days?" He looked at her sideways to see how it would land. She laughed.

"No, I'm a social worker. But I do have a few clients who do sex work. I help at-risk people find housing, make sure they set up bank accounts, cash government cheques, get their rent paid. The sort of stuff that's hard to do when you live precariously. It's actually," she said, "why I'm in town. I have to pick up some court documents for a client of mine."

They walked toward the sound of the helicopter, which moved away. David said, "I thought you were going to be a missionary or something?"

"Oh, God. Yeah. No. I didn't do that. Sort of a long story, but I ended up going to UBC after high school. I was supposed to go to UVic with Laura, but it felt weird going without her, you know? So I went to Vancouver, got a place in residence. The summer after first year, I didn't want to go back to Nanaimo, which is where my parents moved. It wasn't really home, and you remember how they were? After eight months away, I didn't want to go back to that. I was still involved with my church back then, and through them I got a job for the summer working at a mission on the Downtown Eastside. That was an eye-opener. I handed out sandwiches or whatever and prayed and it took, like, maybe three days to see that wasn't helping anyone at all."

"You don't say."

"I mean food helps, of course. But what was really needed was support—housing, money, access to mental health counselling. Without any of that, it's impossible to even start helping, and no one I worked with seemed to be thinking of that. Even outside of the church stuff, everything seemed to be just . . . band-aid solutions. Anyways, that's how I got interested. I switched my majors to focus on social work, then stayed in school for a master's. I worked at a housing society for a decade. Then I moved back to the island. My parents are getting older and need help, and Vancouver is so expensive. So I found a similar sort of job and have been back on the island for the last five years.

"But," she said, "I never really got back here. I mean, I drive through on my way to Victoria, but I never stop. I don't have the connection. My parents weren't from here. We were gone most summers. I mostly hung out with my youth group in Chemainus growing up. When I'd come back to the island to visit, I'd only ever go to Nanaimo. There was never any reason to come back, so I didn't. Until today. And of course, I run into the one person I know here."

"It's that sort of place," David said. "I can't seem

NOT THAT KIND OF PLACE

to go two blocks without running into, like, Becky Anderson."

"Oh, God. Becky. How's she?"

"Of everyone I've known, I would say she's changed the least."

"I'm not surprised."

"You weren't friends?"

"She was more Laura's friend. Honestly, Laura was pretty much my only friend in high school. But she was friends with everyone, you know?"

The helicopter was louder again, but still out of sight. They walked past the old sporting goods store and a new bead shop. David said, "After high school I travelled around the island a lot. I'd hitchhike every-where. My dad hated it. 'My son standing on the side of a highway like a bum,' he'd say, but he wouldn't lend me his car and mine had broken down, so there wasn't much choice. I went to all the towns on the island. Port McNeill, Chemainus, wherever. I really liked Courtenay. It was like bizarro-here—same size, same kids. I would go there and hang out with people who were like the people here but didn't know me at all. Consequently," he told Carolyn, "freed of my D&D-playing past, I was able to get a girlfriend there. But as I got older and I got a car, the appeal of going elsewhere wore out. Being drunk in a town two hours away from my bed became less fun. So, yeah, I don't really go anywhere much on the island either. I go to Victoria sometimes, but nowhere else. I mean, what the hell do I need in Ladysmith?"

"That's fair. But if I hadn't stopped in Griffiths, where would I get my healing crystals?" They were walking by Journeys, a shop that sold mystical rocks and spell books. "I can't believe that's still here."

"I'm almost positive it's the oldest business in town."

"I got in trouble in grade nine for shopping there. Me and Laura had gone on our lunch hour and picked up a couple of crystals and a book about dream interpretation. You'd have thought I brought home a Marilyn Manson record or something, the way my parents reacted." A few shops later, Carolyn said, "At least there are more stores here than there used to be. This used to be mostly empty."

"They've been trying to encourage small business. We've got a hip barbershop now. There's a farmers' market every weekend. A craft brewery. And we're a fashion capital." He pointed to a sign in a dress shop that said, "Milan, New York, Paris, Griffiths."

They had, by then, crossed the four blocks of downtown Griffiths and were at the edge. Shops on one side of the street; on the other, a parking lot backed by woods. A few hundred metres through that was the river and, beyond that, nothing but forest cut through with logging roads for two hundred kilometres until the ocean.

The helicopter was a distant thrum again. Carolyn and David looked down the road, into the trees. They could just see where the black bridge crossed the river.

"It's Jake who they're looking for." A woman sitting on a motorized chair had pulled up alongside them.

David said, "John?"

"Who?"

"John."

"I said Jake. Jake Holmstead. It's who they're looking for. He's been living down on the river for years, under the bridge. He went missing last week but they only started looking today."

The highway crossed the river at the silver bridge. An encampment had grown there. Griffiths had a homeless shelter, but it only had ten beds and no city councillor would approve a bigger place. Every few months, the tarps and tents got cleared out and the encampments would move to the woods for a few weeks before slowly setting up under the bridge again.

"You know how they get there. Drugs. They get in their fights. It's a shame. I knew his parents. He used to work at the mill. Then he started with this girl. No good for him. He got drinking and you know how that is. Probably he got pushed in is what I heard."

Carolyn said, "That's terrible."

"Well, you get into that stuff you get what's coming, you know? But from a good family. What a waste."

Carolyn and David left the woman and walked along the path between the seniors' community and an overgrown ditch that had once been a creek. It brought them to Centennial Park.

The park had tennis courts, a playground, and a large open field. There were a dozen trees at the edge and then a steep embankment up a hill. David had found an arrow there when he was eight. It stuck straight out of the ground like it had been shot down from a cloud. The feathers on the end were bright yellow and red, the tip rounded, for children. He took it home and put two nails into his bedroom wall and laid the arrow across. He hadn't thought of that in years and wondered where it had ended up. A half-dozen tents were set up where he'd found the arrow, tarps strung over trees, plastic chairs in the middle.

He and Carolyn hadn't spoken since they'd left the woman on the scooter. David thought about telling her about the arrow for something to say, but before he could she said, "It always felt weird that my family just moved away after the funeral. Like, we never said goodbye or anything."

David said, "My mom never mentioned being bothered by it."

"We had been planning to move before Laura died. My parents, I mean; me and Laura were going to Victoria. My mom worked in Nanaimo and was tired of the commute, so they were only sticking it out until I was done school. With everything going on, I never mentioned it to your mom. I thought my mom would have—I didn't know until after the move she hadn't. But, it made sense, I guess, since our parents never got along."

David said, "Our parents didn't get along?"

"Oh, God no."

"I had no idea. Was it because we didn't go to church?"

"It wasn't so much church as that my dad is an ass-hole," she said.

"Mine was, too. You'd think, with that in common, they'd have been friends."

They sat at a picnic table. Carolyn popped the lid off her coffee cup and started picking at the rim. She said, "I think they might have gotten along fine when we were really young, but by middle school they stopped pretending to like each other. Laura and I got into some trouble and my dad blamed Laura."

"I actually think I remember that. You guys were at a drug party or something?"

"Sort of. We had been invited to a party with Staci Greene, remember her?"

"She was banned from our house after that."

"She wasn't the sort of kid parents were happy to have over, no. The only reason we knew her was

117

because Laura did a project with her in science class or something, and Laura was always good at making friends, so she got invited and I went along. It took a lot of convincing for my parents to let me go, but it was Laura and we'd never gotten into any trouble before. And of course," Carolyn said, "the one time I go to a party led to me never being allowed to go to another. We got there and, like, ten minutes in some kids started doing whippits and Stefani Driscoll freaked out and thought she was going to die and called for a ride home, and then the Driscolls called all the other parents to tell them what was going on at the party and that was that."

"It was whippits? The way my parents reacted I always thought it had to be acid or better."

"My parents were also not big on drug hierarchy," she said. "They still think coffee is pretty much cocaine. The upshot was," Carolyn went on, "my dad blamed Laura for bringing me into a den of iniquity. He thought Laura was heading down a dangerous path and becoming a bad influence on their innocent, God-fearing daughter. And through the transitive property, the blame for Laura fell on your parents."

"I cannot believe that my sister was considered a bad influence by anyone."

"My parents had no idea who Staci was. They just needed to blame someone."

A tennis ball bounced out of the court between them and the fence. David waved that he would get it. Walked across the grass and picked it up. He tossed it over and walked back.

David asked, "Whatever happened to Staci?"

"She dropped out in grade twelve. Left town for a while, I think, but lives here again. Teaches yoga. Has an annoying Instagram with inspirational quotes."

"You're still friends?"

"I have been known to google people from my past."

"I do that, too. Fun fact: my high school bully is in jail for manslaughter. He punched a guy for being gay, the guy fell back into a curb and went into a coma, and died a few weeks later."

"That's awful. Chad Doskel?"

"Chad Doskel is the top BMW salesperson in Austria. The manslaughterer is Travis Robertson. I had several bullies."

"Right—you got duct-taped?"

"Twice. But I always hope no one remembers that."

"Sorry."

"It's okay. I was what was known as a 'nerd,' and as such, expected that kind of treatment."

"People are so awful."

"I'm over it. I hardly ever look at my People-to-Kill list anymore."

They got up and threw their coffee cups in a trash

bin. They walked into town and past the Rainbow. Sue was smoking in the back alley. David waved. She lifted her chin slightly. Carolyn checked her phone.

She said, "I should be getting back. I've got to stop at the cop shop on my way out of town and who knows how long that will take."

"Trouble with the law?"

"For a client. More of a favour than an official duty. She got into some trouble here and her stuff ended up with the cops. She didn't want to go back in for it when she was here because cops tend to not treat people like her real good."

"No?"

"If you're marginalized and put yourself in a cop's vision there's always a chance you end up in jail."

"I guess I never gave that any thought."

"That's because you've never had to. I mean, you're the sort of person who can get away with anything."

"That's not true. Cops were always harassing us for smoking pot or drinking."

"Sure, but did they ever actually do anything to you beyond hassling?"

David thought about it and said, "One time a cop came up to dump my booze outside of the community centre and I smashed the bottle on the ground and told him to fuck off and he just told my friends to get me home."

"Now imagine literally anyone else doing that." David acknowledged she was correct with a shrug. She said, "I mean, my client got beat up by a guy, and instead of being brought to a hospital she was put in jail for the night. The cops finally brought her to get looked over in the morning, and when the hospital discharged her she was there, alone, without any of her things and had to figure out a way to get home to Nanaimo on her own after she was released. And then the cops tell the world she's a sex worker and wash their hands of doing anything about it."

"Your client is that hooker at the farm?"

"Sex worker, David."

"Right, I didn't mean—"

"I know you didn't." And then, immediately, "Sorry. I get worked up about it. I mean, it's my job. I'm always dealing with it and not a lot of people care, so when I'm talking to someone who might actually get it, I press a little."

"I will never say the H-word again."

"It's just frustrating to see it in action. The police can say it was a 'hooker' in a fight over drugs and then everyone thinks, 'Oh, probably had it coming,' and then no one cares anymore. As though being a sex worker means you can get locked up in a house for three days. It's terrible. But I shouldn't be talking about any of this."

"My lips are sealed," David said. "The whole story seems so wild. I'm surprised to find out there's sex workers in town, I guess."

"There has always been sex work in this town."

"Really?"

"Really."

In grade twelve, David had been waiting with a girl he had a crush on for the Greyhound to take her home. She lived in Chemainus; it was a short ride, but the only way to get from town to town on the island. While they waited, a truck pulled up and the driver rolled down his window and said, "Do you know where I can get some company?" He looked David's friend up and down. The Greyhound station was just a bench, a payphone, and a door with the Greyhound logo on it that only opened to sell tickets ten minutes before the bus came and closed twenty minutes after the bus had been unloaded. David missed the meaning, so the guy added, "A girl, you know. Company." David still wasn't sure and was surprised when the girl he was with said, "Fuck off, I'm calling the cops." The guy left in a hurry and David asked what was going on and the girl said, "That guy was looking for *a girl* and thought I was one." David was sure she had misunderstood something, because that sort of thing didn't happen in that town, and she couldn't believe he thought it was nothing — "What if I'd been alone? What if he'd been more aggressive?" she kept asking—and then the bus pulled in and she got on it.

David said, "Never really realized, I guess, but you're probably right."

"It's always been everywhere."

They waited at the light under the GO TURDS sign. The light changed and they crossed to their cars. Carolyn said, "That reporter you mentioned. It's about Laura?"

David had forgotten that he'd let that slip. He said, "Yeah."

"Almost twenty years. They must have an alert for these things."

"I've thought that myself."

"I was asked for interviews a few times, in the years after, but always said no. Are you talking to him?"

"My mom was. I don't know. I'm kind of surprised she was talking to him. She got burned by this thing a few years ago."

"That podcast?"

"No, it was a TV show. But the podcast used clips from the TV show, I think."

"God."

"Yeah. So I'm surprised she was talking to anyone. She seemed to think the guy was sincere, but it's like, fool me once, shame on you, or whatever. I don't know. This guy wrote mostly about yuppies making their houses nicer until recently. Seems like he's trying to make a name for himself or something. I honestly don't care one way or the other if he does it. I just don't want to be bothered about it, you know?"

"Well then, if he gets in touch with me I'll tell him to fuck off."

They both laughed. She said she'd be back in town to pick up some court documents for her client in a few days. She wondered if it would be okay to give him a call.

"I've been staying in my mom's part of the house. You can call the landline, it's—"

She said the number.

"You remember."

"I called it every day for twelve years."

"Right. Well, if I don't pick up, try again. There's no voice mail or anything and I've been missing a lot of calls."

"Will do. I'm happy I bumped into you."

"I am too."

CHAPTER ELEVEN

AFTER CAROLYN LEFT, DAVID sat in his mom's car. He had nothing to do; packing wasn't urgent and being home meant the reporter could find him. He pulled out, onto the highway, then turned off onto the old sideroads.

In grade twelve social studies, Mr. Jameson showed David's class a map of Griffiths Valley from pioneer times — 1860 or so. He had put it on a transparency and projected it onto the wall. The shoreline, river, and lakes were all recognizable. The First Nation settlements were marked. He pointed out the white-people trading posts near the bays. At the time it was easier to get around by water, he explained. You could sail from Fuller's Bay to Sidney, outside of Victoria, in a couple of hours, but crossing the mountains overland would have taken days. The major inland trails were marked as well. They had been used by Indigenous people for centuries. When the government surveyors came to make this map, they'd used those trails and local guides to survey the valley.

He laid a second map, from early 1900, over the first. Lumber mills appeared along the rivers, farms on the river estuary lands. He showed them how the trails from the first map had become the first roads. He explained how resources — trees mostly, but there had also been some mining — were taken from inland along the roads and brought to Fuller's Bay to be shipped around the world. Those roads meandered along the contours of the land, then cut straight into the woods where access was needed. Around the town's two lakes and the river floodplain, a grid of roads had been put in to access the new farms.

When he put the third map down, he asked if they saw anything different. This one was from 1920. By 1905, he told the class, the railway had been built. Because it didn't make sense for the rail to follow the shoreline to the existing bay villages, it cut straight through, east of the settlements. Robert Griffiths, whom the town was named after, had built his own station along the line to get the train to stop. He was tired of having to navigate the bad roads to Fuller's Bay to drop off his supplies. The town grew around Griffith's Station, adopted the name of the stop and then dropped the "Station" and the apostrophe. Mr. Jameson said it was only because capitalism dictated the rail line that connected the settlements on the island be made straight and cheap, and because a farmer had the capital and clout to make a train stop, that a town existed here at all.

He laid down a fourth map, from after the Second World War. He showed how the new highway had been built to follow the rail line — blasted through, rather than built to the land. It saved a half-hour commuting time by destroying the mountain, rather than follow the centuries-old paths that had been built around the natural features of the island and mountains.

He said, "We came here and settled. We took what we could and tore the land apart to move it around our needs. None of it for the profit of anyone who lived here, but all of it going back to the Hudson's Bay Company or the logging corporations in Ontario or England. We destroyed the land, turned raw forest into tree farms. Ruined the rivers. All for commodity removal. The only reason a city is here at all is because a farmer didn't want to hitch his buggy and go to the next station down the line. The entitlement of it all is something you kids should know. It's all stolen land, justified by white supremacy."

The school board fired Mr. Jameson later that year; he had already been warned to tone down his lectures.

He now ran as an independent candidate in provincial elections and never got more than a couple dozen votes.

David's takeaway from the lecture had been a curiosity about the old trails that became the roads. He noticed that Sherman Road, which Mountain came off of, had been built over the trail that connected two of the First Nation bands, and that Sherman changed names but never seemed to end, winding its way off the edge of the maps.

He told his dad he had a school project to work on and borrowed the car the next weekend. David and a friend started in Shawnigan Lake and decided to follow the road that had been built over the trails as far as they could north. They knew much of the route between Shawnigan and David's house; the road followed the river through the reserve and then out to Fuller's Bay. There, it curved inland again, crossed the highway. David had driven along parts of the route before — to friend's houses and on family drives — but had never realized the sections of the road that connected. His dad would never have taken a meandering back road scenic route when the highway went right to where they were going.

When they got close to David's house, they turned onto the highway. Sherman ended in a dead end — the old German couple had lobbied the city to block highway access; before that, drivers would use Sherman as a shortcut between the new and old highway, driving like they were still on a highway, which endangered their grandkids—but the road resumed on the other side, with a different name. David figured out the back roads to get there and then was driving in new territory.

The road took them over and along creeks and rivers and past houses he'd never seen. A sign said "Everhome," which he learned was an old train stop that was considered part of Griffiths, but technically could have been its own town. The road wound by the old mill, then through the next town to the north. Sometimes he'd recognize a building or a stretch of road, but once they were north of Chemainus, everything was new. The road took them along the ocean, through little towns he'd only known as signs on the highway. They stopped in them to look around and pop into thrift stores, and then kept on going. They passed the old drive-in outside of Nanaimo. It had stopped showing movies by then, but his dad had taken the family to a Sunday flea market there a few years before.

David was talking about the road taking them all the way to Cape Scott at the northern tip of the island when they came around a corner to find a private road with a gate. The property was owned by a company named Stelcor, which, a sign told them, had not had a workplace injury in over a year.

They took the highway back, forty minutes by straight shot, but three hours the way they'd taken out. That night, David's dad asked him how he managed to put 250 kilometres on his car and David wasn't allowed to drive it again.

When David got his own car, he'd spend weekends driving the old routes with friends. They'd drive to Courtenay or Lake Cowichan or Port Alberni and find odd places. Surprising views, waterfalls, abandoned buildings, large industrial plants. Old sites they found on maps that were nothing but a dead end or trees. They'd park at them and drink, then drive home along the highway. It was something to do.

It had been years now since he'd driven the back roads. He followed the river all the way inland to Lake Cowichan, then turned onto the logging roads. The dirt road had trees close on either side; it went up and then down and to a sudden view of the river canyon, then back up. He slowed down on corners—his van had come with a CB radio, so when he was young he'd been able to hear the logging trucks call out where they were, to avoid getting hit by them. The CB had broken years before and he'd never bothered to replace it. And now he was in his mom's car anyways. He didn't see any trucks, but a group of ATVers drove by and waved to him.

Coming back into town over Pole Hill, he hit a clear-cut that was new. He was high enough to see the whole valley in the distance. A haze around the highway, two small lakes, the shallow one more green than blue. The river cut through the middle to the ocean, which he could just barely see at Fuller's Bay.

The logging road brought him back to town. He drove through and turned off the main roads again on the other side, heading toward the ocean. The road went into the reserve, which was on the river's tributary land. There was no shoulder and trees grew right over it. It crossed the arms of the river on small wooden bridges. The river was diked through town, but here it flooded in heavy rain or even high tide, when the ocean pushed it to run backwards. It was swampy where it had not been built up. Mount McAllister, the other big mountain that marked the south edge of the valley, dominated the skyline. It stuck out into Fuller's Bay, dropping straight into the ocean.

David drove past the old missionary church and the unfinished stone church on the hill, and then around a tight curve, then came to a line of cars pulled alongside the shoulder before a bridge. He stopped in time but the gravel crunching startled a few people. They were lined up all along one side of the bridge. As he crossed the bridge he saw a metal boat going down the river. There were two cops in it and one in hip waders, a few feet into the river, talking to the two in the boat.

He rolled down the window to ask what was up.

"Looking for Jake Holmstead. Heard he fell in the river taking a piss up by Paradise." Paradise was a swimming spot up the river, on the west side of the canyon, where David had heard the helicopter.

"Any sign of him?"

"Nah. Probably made it out to the bay. Might find his foot next year." David drove over the bridge and kept going, slow now through the curves.

Feet had been washing up on the inside shore of the island every year. They were always in shoes. Bodies in water floated into the strait and sank. But over time the shoes, being buoyant, lifted the feet to the surface, where the current dropped them along the island. A person would walk up and kick or poke the shoe or their dog would drop it at their feet or gnaw on it and they'd realize there was bone sticking out. In the last eight years, more than a dozen had been found, none matching. People had worried after the first three or four, but now it had become a novelty — a News of the Weird sort of thing. Some kids had even faked one. They put a leg bone from a horse in an old Converse and left it above the high-tide line.

Three people had been identified though DNA. They'd all lived on the streets in the Downtown Eastside of Vancouver. It was assumed they'd killed themselves by jumping off the Lions Gate or Second Narrows Bridge, but some people thought it was murder. A serial killer had worked for years in the Downtown Eastside. He got away with it for so long because his victims were sex workers and the police couldn't be bothered to follow up on any of the leads they got, including from a woman who had just barely escaped being killed and told the police, in detail, what this guy had going on. That guy was in jail, but another killer could do it just as easy, knowing the police weren't looking into that sort of thing.

The only reason anyone had heard anything about Carolyn's client was because she got away. If she hadn't, David thought, maybe a foot would have turned up years later and everyone would have thought she just killed herself.

The reserve ended at the lawn tennis club, the oldest surviving business in town. Two of the first farms in town were there too, and a stand of old-growth trees. They were in a field between the club and the bay, about three dozen of them. Moss hung down from the branches. Branches fell off regularly. Three were just stumps. You could buy a picture postcard of them in town. In the fall, people would sit at the tennis club to paint the trees.

David waited for his turn at the four-way stop. He'd been planning to head back to Griffiths for some food, but decided at the last minute to go straight, following the curve of the ocean into Fuller's Bay.

CHAPTER TWELVE

THE CAT FISH CAFÉ was empty except for the waitress. She looked up from behind the counter and told David to sit wherever he wanted.

"Is the patio open?"

"It is if you get your own chair."

They were stacked against a wall on the narrow deck that wrapped around two sides of the building, over the water. David took one and put it under the awning and then flipped one plastic table off another and put it in place. The waitress came out with a menu and wiped the table.

She said, "Wasn't expecting it to be this warm, otherwise I'd have set it up myself. Get you a drink?" He asked what kind of beers they had, and she said, "We

got them all. Coors. Canadian. Kokanee." He asked for
a Kokanee.

Mount McAllister rose up out of the opposite side
of the bay. It was sheer where the mountain went into
the water, rock grey and dark. Halfway between David
and the mountain, a deep dock stuck out into the bay.
A crane loaded a freighter with lumber stacked there
in piles as tall as houses. Closer, on the docks that stuck
out below the restaurant, a man in a T-shirt and toque
washed the deck of his sailboat.

Fuller's Bay was only ten minutes from Griffiths
and considered part of the town, but David hadn't been
there in years. The only business he'd recognized driving through the village was the Cat Fish. The sign was
the same—a fish with a hook through its mouth. There
had been a rumour in high school that the restaurant
was a cover for drug smuggling, and if you ordered
the daily catch and put your money on the table, you
would get a fish with a brick of cocaine hidden in it. By
the time David was old enough to get in with a fake
ID, it was just a regular blue-collar bar. The first couple
of years after high school, David would go there to
"slum it," but by then the fishing industry was mostly
gone and the men at the bar were locals who owned
sailboats.

The waitress said, "Here's your Coors," and asked
what he'd like to eat.

David ordered and said, "This place has changed since I was last here."

"You grow up around here?"

"North of Griffiths. But I'd come here a lot when I was young."

"Sure, it's changed a lot. I've been working here since ninety-six." She looked up. "Or maybe ninety-five? Five owners ago, anyways. I started when the Gaffigans owned it, and they had sold it by ninety-seven, so it must have been ninety-six." David nodded. "The sons took it over and there was a fight—you know how it is with inheritances and sons. Anyways, they ended up selling it to Richard North, who owns the deep dock. Then he got into some money trouble and sold off a lot of the things he'd invested in. A couple other guys gave it a shot and now it's owned by some outfit in Vancouver. I've never met the new owners, but they have this 'manager' they send by and he's got all these ideas. They're changing everything. The restaurant has been here fifty years and they want to change things? Can you believe that?"

She unhooked a small, flat screen from her belt and showed it to David. "I'm supposed to put my orders in this thing. I've been using this notepad for twenty years and it hasn't failed me yet. So now what I have to do is write down the order and then go inside and figure out how to punch it in here so this stupid machine can send a message two feet to the kitchen. It's ridiculous. And get this." She smiled. "They call it a POS system. And that's just what it is. A real P-O-S." She laughed.

"Anyways, I know things need to be improved — this place was a real shithole and is better now, for sure — but you can't just go around changing for the sake of changing. My regulars had been coming here since before I worked here. You mess with the menu, you're going to lose them. People won't be loyal to you if you're not loyal to them."

David said, "Yeah, Griffiths is the same way. I work out at the —"

She said, "Oh yeah, one sec," and went back into the restaurant, tapping at her screen.

An orange whale-watching boat started its engine. There were maybe a dozen people in it, all wearing yellow ponchos. It pulled out of the docks and then gunned its engine. The sound echoed back from the cliffs across the bay. David watched its wake spread, out past the deep dock and freighter, then between Salt Spring Island and Mount McAllister. The sound stopped when the boat disappeared around the bay. Water lapped against the docks. When David was young, his family would come here sometimes and Laura and David would run around the docks, looking at the boats and into the water to see jellyfish and starfish stuck to the dock pilings. David looked over the patio rail. A rainbow oil slick swayed on the water's surface. He could not see the bottom.

The waitress put a burger down on the table. David said, "Could you really buy cocaine here back in the day?"

She snorted. "Yeah. Order white fish to go, hand over a hundred bucks, and you'd get a fish with a bag of coke in it." She added, "That was before my time though."

"I always thought that was an urban legend."

"You're probably too young to remember, but this used to be a real rough place. Not just the restaurant, the whole village. During fishing season, it was like a boom town. Boats would go out and come back with these huge catches. Buyers would show up with a brief-case full of money and guys with guns to guard them. The skipper split the cash up with the crew. Everyone had these huge rolls. The hotels couldn't handle it, so guys slept on boats or wherever they could. There were six bars—you could get anything at them back then. Drugs and girls or whatever."

"Girls?"

"Oh yeah. The bikers had some local girls they'd get to go out on the boats. And you had peelers too, over from Vancouver."

"Really."

"You looking for something?"

"No, no, no. I just didn't know."

"It was that kind of place back then. You know, some of the guys who went out fishing went over the border and come back with a boatload of coke under some fish. No one I knew. But you hear things. Anyways, the Cat Fish was run by bikers, and they snuck the drugs in with the catch of the day. Before my time — that owner was long gone by the time I started here. Got killed."

"Really?"

"Yeah, they mailed his head to the bikers' clubhouse up island."

"Jesus."

"They never did find the body."

"Did his feet turn up?"

"Feet? No, just the head."

David sipped his beer. The waitress said, "I guess he owed people money, and it was just that kind of place back then. You wouldn't believe the kind of things that went on here. People killed and you never heard about it. The drugs bring that kind of thing.

"There was a house up the east arm of the river from the bay. It was way back from the ocean, but shallow, you know, like in the estuary. Really overgrown and swampy. The owner cut a path through it you could sneak a boat up. A few times a week a float plane would come in from the US. They'd land on that side at night, drop a buoy, then float over to the government dock like they were just coming in for the night. A boat would come out from the house and pick up the buoy. Everyone knew what was going on because the plane landing at night was as loud as anything.

"Anyways, the guy who owned the place and his wife got killed. Three guys broke in and tied them up, shotgun to the head. Real messy. Had to be identified by their fingerprints, you know what I mean? I was a kid then, coming home from school, and saw two police helicopters over the bay. I guess a neighbour heard the shots and called the cops. There's only one road out on that side of the bay, so they ran into the cops driving out, turned around and got chased back to the house, then made a run for it. Two of them got into the boat they used for the nighttime pickups, and the other guy decided to go over the mountain. I saw the two guys in the boat come out of the river and a huge Coast Guard boat came around into the bay. They'd been doing some training out by Salt Spring and got the call. The guys in the boat got forced to beach over by Shanty Cove and got picked up a little later. The guy who went over the mountain never got caught. I'd always heard it was somehow tied up with this place, but like I said, it was all before my time."

David said, "Jesus," again.

"But you don't get much of that here anymore. It's a nice place now."

David said, "I don't know, on my way out here—"

She looked inside and said, "One sec."

A couple with two kids were inside, waiting to be seated. They motioned to the window. She sat them where they could look out at the bay, which was on the other side of the glass from David. One of the kids waved at him; he waved back. The waitress brought them crayons for their placemats, and David shifted his chair so his back was to them.

After he finished his food, David walked down the ramp to the docks. A few more people were out on their boats. He went out to the end of one dock, then back, then down another. On the main dock that ran parallel to the shore there were houseboats, not the ship-like things he remembered from when he was young, but vinyl-sided, suburban-looking houses that happened to be floating. There was a laundromat with public showers; he had gotten a good peacoat from the lost and found there years before. There was only socks and a pair of pants in it now. From the end of the concrete dock with the gas station, he looked back at the village. The buildings had all been painted bright colours. It looked like a postcard of the Maritimes.

David went past the government dock and was surrounded by work boats. Fishing boats, a couple of tugs. There was a covered dry dock on the beach. A worker pressure-washed barnacles off a hull. The boats were all flat, stainless steel. They had large drums to roll in nets. One or two had clothes drying off the rigging— people must live on them. There weren't many, but he supposed that fishing season was off, not that he knew anything about it. This looked more like the place he remembered.

A girl hopped off one of the boats and walked by David, her arms wrapped up in a thin hoody that wasn't right for the weather. An older man came out of the cabin and nodded to David. At the end of the dock David looked over the water, past the deep dock at the mountain.

He passed the girl on his way back. She had a bag with a loaf of bread in it and a coffee in the other hand. She looked down at the dock when she passed. David walked back up the ramp and to his car.

CHAPTER THIRTEEN

DAVID GOT HOME AFTER the sun had gone down. He'd driven the old roads along the ocean all the way to Nanaimo, and then come back into town from the north, straight along the highway. The double bump of the mountain wasn't visible coming from that direction; it was just a lump of rock and trees, indistinguishable from any other. The highway went around the bottom. David turned off and wound his way around the base and home.

David had put the Laura box on the kitchen table. When he came up the stairs, it was the first thing he saw. He poured himself a glass of water and stared at it.

His mom had written NEWSPAPER CLIPPINGS on the top folder. The clippings were ordered from most recent to oldest. The first few were printouts from the CBC website. The articles came out at the time of the *Not That Kind of Place* documentary and were written to promote it. They all said basically the same thing—Laura McPherson, killed at eighteen, murder unsolved. Her grad picture at the top of the article; halfway down the article, the award-winning picture of David's dad and the stretcher with her body coming out of the woods. A mugshot of Greg Dykma under the subhead "Retired detective fingers neighbour in new documentary." There were some quotes from a Detective Coulson, taken from the documentary, about how they had questioned Dykma but how difficult it was, and how not being able to get a conviction was the great failing of Coulson's career.

The subhead "A history of criminal behaviour" came before a short biography of Dykma. He'd done some petty crimes. A cousin had gotten him the job on the gravel pit. There were no charges the four years he lived there. And then the accusation. He left town, was charged with break-and-enters in Kamloops, and then a series of minor charges to do with loitering and trespassing. He died in a Medicine Hat rooming house of an overdose that was assumed to be suicide.

David had been in his basement suite playing video games when he found out. His dad came down through the laundry room. David said, "I told you, you have to knock." His dad said, "Greg Dykma died." David kept playing. His dad stood there. David didn't look over or pause the game and, after a couple of minutes, his dad left. He died a couple of months later. David would always feel bad that that was the last time they'd spoken.

The article closed with quotes from his mom. The same edited ones from the documentary. "He will have to live with what he did..." She meant whoever did it, but as in the show, the quote was positioned to look like she meant Dykma.

The next printouts in the folder were from the tenth anniversary of Laura's death. CBC articles, a longer thing in *Maclean's*. Recaps, quotes from his uncle — "We pray every day that justice will come, but it is in God's hands." Anyone with information was asked to call. David worked backwards through time. The fifth anniversary, the third, the first. All variations of the same thing. And then articles from when the investigation was in progress.

After Laura's body was found, David's dad stopped bringing home newspapers, and the case was never talked about in front of David. To get news, David had to sneak the paper home or, once he was back in school, read the local paper at the Rainbow or the coffee shop while skipping. It only took him reading the first few words of the clipped articles to remember the whole article. Police still searching for leads in the murder of. A person of interest questioned in the case of. In the days after a local girl, a hiker, believed she may have seen. No new information on. Today, the funeral of. A funeral planned for. A sad conclusion to the case of. The search continues for. Searchers gather at. A Discman thought to belong to. No new information in the. A girl missing in a town an hour north of.

David closed the file and put it beside the box.

The next folder had UNSOLVED CANADA written on it. It was filled with bundles of computer paper stapled in the top corner — some were two pages, other twelve or more. David couldn't make sense of what he was looking at. Sentences cut off and started a line down; there were pictures with dates that seemed unrelated to anything, and lines at random running around the page. It took looking through three bundles before he realized they were printouts of message boards. His mom must have hit Print Screen, but the formatting of the pages online didn't make it to the printer.

He went back to the first bundle. The thread had been posted by someone named "PewterSocks," which was the name of his mom's first cat and her screen name on Candy Crush. She'd written, "Looking for any updates on the post from 2006 of the murdered girl in Griffiths, BC . . . Someone had thought there might be a tie-in to a similar murder in Nelson three years later . . . Anyone have more?" The five pages after were the responses. A few links to articles David had just read in the newspaper folders, and a couple of conspiracy theories linking his sister's murder to the Green River Killer and another to the pig farmer in Vancouver. Someone connected both murders to a guy who'd robbed, and then jumped out of, a plane in the 1970s.

The next bundle was a thread titled "Any news in the death of Laura McPherson." It hadn't been posted by his mom, but she'd written the first comment: "I'd like to hear more too please." David flipped through the other packages in the folder and then took out the next folder, UNSOLVED CANADA 2. Under it, UNSOLVED CANADA 3 and then 4, and then MYSTERY HUNTERS 1 and 2, SOLVEIT, UNSOLVED, and COLD CASE 1–3.

When the Walmart David worked at was still in the town mall, his mom would ask him to refill her printer cartridges. There was an ink jet kiosk at the mall entrance. David would drop the cartridges off on his way into work and pick them up on the way out. He had asked her what she was printing so much of, and she said it was nothing much, just some news stories she wanted to keep. David tried to tell her that they'd always be online, but she said she liked to have them. He did this for at least a year, and then she asked less and less, so he didn't notice when it stopped.

The most recent post he found was from six years before; the next newest was a year before that. Most of her posts were from a period of three years, starting in 2005. The oldest comment from his mom he could find was October 21, 2005. Right after his dad died. She commented on a thread started three years before, titled "Main suspect in McPherson Case Suicide: Guilt or something else?" On the third page, a year after the previous comment, his mom had posted: "I know the theory is that Greg Dykma did it but it never made any sense to me . . . Why would he kill a neighbour? Any other theories?" Someone responded, pointing her to an earlier thread.

That post was a few bundles down: "Laura McPherson, Murdered Griffiths Girl. Solved? A Theory," posted by IslandBoi420. He outlined what was public record — the days she was missing followed by the discovery of the Discman on the logging road and how her body was eventually found by her own dad — and then went into more detail. The post had to be ten thousand words. The poster thought the local police must have had something to do with it. A number of women in the valley had gone missing over the years. They were not as widely reported as Laura's case because they were part of the local First Nation. As near as IslandBoi420 could tell, the police had barely looked into any of the missing women until Laura went missing and "A middle class white family raised a fuss." His theory was that the police were covering up something they were doing, or a crooked cop (or more than one) was covering up for the local bikers, who they had ties with. He referenced the pig farmer in Vancouver. Further, two of the officers involved in the initial investigation were, years later, accused of sexual assault in different cases. They had both been transferred out of town shortly after Laura's murder. He posted links to articles backing up everything he said. He had tracked down a payroll for the local police department to back up his claims that they had been accused of assault later. He had even demonstrated ties between police and the bikers by showing that, after one of the officers retired, he had gone into business with the wife of a biker. The business was in her maiden name, but the poster connected it with marriage records and her husband's criminal record, which was one charge of possession in the late eighties. The business was to maintain logging roads. In conclusion, the poster realized it was circumstantial, but thought it warranted a deeper look.

The first comment after IslandBoi420's five-page investigation was, "Nice work, lots to think of." There were a few more comments along those lines. Someone said that that sounded like the pigs. And then someone pointed out that while they agreed Dykma doing it was unlikely and that the police were covering up, he thought it was their incompetence they were covering, not wrongdoing. The poster wrote, "Never attribute to malice that which is adequately explained by incompetence." Another poster went further, saying it wasn't incompetence so much as systemic racism — they linked to a government report about missing and murdered Indigenous women and pointed out that the four girls other than Laura who had gone missing were from the reserve. The police didn't search for them because they didn't care; the papers didn't follow up on them because they didn't care either. The next poster said he'd been with the force for a decade and had never seen anything like racism — just people who wanted to do right. The next poster said if the previous poster didn't see racism in the force, it was because he was probably a racist. The thread devolved from there.

The next bundle of papers had another theory. And then, another theory after that. And another. And another. David read the first dozen closely, then started scanning them. Some theories were plausible — a lot of them tied the police to the bikers; David realized pretty quickly that IslandBoi420 had put his post together using bits and pieces of other posts, uncredited. Others were less likely. Some people tried to give themselves an air of knowledge — "I'm a retired investigator from Kansas," "As a forensic pathologist from Winnipeg" — but their knowledge obviously came from CSI. There

152

were lots of "Cops covering for cops," a few "Laura Palmer situation," and one "Anyone looked into the brother?" There were hundreds of pages of this.

David plugged in the rotary phone and looked through the years-old phone book for a pizza place he knew was still open. He called in an order and then pulled everything else out. At the bottom was a VHS tape. A folded note to his mom tucked inside on the letterhead of the Victoria news station read, *Here's the newscast footage regarding your daughter. I hope this can bring you some comfort.* Under that, loose paper, a handbill from the funeral, copies of Laura's missing posters—the one Becky and the girls from the yearbook committee had made, and the police one. A copy of his sister's grad yearbook with signatures from her whole class. Funeral remembrances, a bill for her funeral, with WAIVED stamped across it.

The pizza arrived and David went back to the message board posts, working his way slowly through it all.

CHAPTER FOURTEEN

KNOCKING WOKE DAVID UP the next morning. He'd
fallen asleep on the couch with the blinds open; the
rising sun shone in on him. He had sweat through
his T-shirt and the pillow was soaked. He sat up. The
grinding noise started in the kitchen and Becky's head
appeared in the bottom corner of the big living room
window. Her cellphone was up at her ear; the other
hand shaded her eyes so she could see in. She jumped
back, then waved, when she saw David staring at her.

David went down and opened the side door. Becky
looked uncertainly at him. David said, "I just woke up,
give me a minute."

"I've been up since six. I had to take my youngest
to soccer practice. The early mornings are annoying,

but I'm trying to enjoy them since Laura is going to move out soon, too." She stepped in and took her jacket off, hung it on the hook. Slipped her shoes off. She said, "You remember my oldest, Chad? He's already gone. Moved to Nanaimo for school. Trev has taken a year off to earn some money and was thinking he would get a welding ticket, like his dad. I don't know about that. It's such hard work and takes you all over, but you know, everyone needs to make their own path in life. But, like I was saying, Laura is probably going to get a scholarship for soccer, which would help with college but means she's probably moving away. It's all hard now, but I'll miss it when they're gone."

David said, "I just woke up, give me a minute."

He left her in the living room and went to the upstairs bathroom to give himself some space. He used the toilet and ran the shower. The water came out rusty for a minute before it turned clear. His mom had an ensuite bathroom, so no one had used this one in years. He found a two-litre bottle of "European formula" no-name shampoo and a dried cake of soap in the shower. The towel was scratchy and started to smell like mould after it got wet. He put on the clothes he'd been wearing and went downstairs.

Becky smiled at him from the armchair. David went into the kitchen and put on the coffee.

Becky said, "Are you moving?"

David had left a stack of empty boxes in the living room, but had so far put only a couple of knick-knacks and a large marbled bowl he'd always hated in them. He said, "Just getting rid of some stuff."

"It's so strange to see the house any different. It's always been such a comfort to me that it was always the same. I know you felt that way too," she told David. "Your mom always said how you didn't like change; she told me how upset you were when they turned your old room into an office."

"Do you want a coffee?"

"Your mom has a box of Passion Tango tea she keeps for me."

David opened the cupboard to show her he'd thrown everything out. "I guess coffee would be fine then. With sugar and milk?"

David had neither. She said she could try it black. "It might be interesting to try."

Everything poured, they sat across from each other in the living room. Becky drew in a slow breath and prepared.

"I think it's important for us to remain in touch. There are less and less links to Laura, and we are bound by that. I wanted to honour Laura's memory and your mother's wishes. But I realize the timing of what I asked of you was bad.

"One of the things I've been working on," she said, "is seeing the two sides of things. I know you and I deal differently with trauma, but I forgot to change my expectations based on who I was talking to. This is a problem I've always had. It's something I worked on in my marriage. And it's something I need to work on in my friendships. I should have approached you differently."

David waited to see if that was it. Then said, "You and Trevor broke up."

"What?"

"You said you worked on it in your marriage. Seems like maybe it didn't work so well?"

"Yes, but I can see, now, more of his perspective," Becky said. "Have you ever been in therapy?" She kept going before David could answer. "The thing I had to confront was my own part in the failure of our marriage. I always blamed Trevor. But we had this... it's called codependence. The whole relationship was my idea, you know. At the time, I said grief brought us together. But the truth was that Trevor and Laura had only been dating for a month; they were never that close, and it probably wouldn't have worked out. Trevor was put into the role of grieving boyfriend. He was sad, of course, but it wasn't like they'd been friends for years, like Laura and I. And Trevor just went along with it. He even said, a few times, that if I didn't want to keep going, that was fine. But any time he said that, I felt even worse and held him even closer."

David looked out the window. A goose had landed on the lawn and was waddling toward the ditch.

"We got married after the first baby, and maybe that was a mistake, too, but what else were we supposed to do? I beat myself up over that for too many years—I accept, now, that it was the decision we had to make at the time. After Chad, Trevor got a job and we could move out of my mom's house and we thought that would make things better. We were adults, out on our own. We had two kids and a job that paid well. But we were nineteen," she said. "Nineteen.

"Trevor's job took him away a lot. He wanted to move the family to Fort Mac, but I didn't want to live where I didn't know anyone. And he worked long days—it wasn't like we'd see each other more anyways. By then we had Laura too and we were just so settled here...

"If you think about it," she said, "in the seventeen years we were together we really only spent maybe five years physically together. And what therapy did for me was to show me how to see things from Trevor's perspective. He behaved like a jerk, but he was in a situation he didn't like either, alone and working for a family he never saw, and who, when he did, didn't live up to what he expected from a family. The kids barely knew him to miss him. And I can see now that I was miserable too, but didn't know it. When you don't know anything else, there's no way to know things aren't as good as they can be.

"I'm happier now," Becky said. "My oldest is in college, Laura is graduating this year. I'm almost forty, single, about to be child-free. It's like a new start. I'm looking forward to the future for the first time in a long time."

David said, "That's really great for you."

"Thanks for saying so. It's been a long journey, but I feel like I'm coming out of something." She considered a moment. "I've also been reconsidering the ways I've mourned your sister. You know, James has been helping me process that. It's nice to have someone to talk to about Laura, someone who didn't know her, but who wants to know more. I can talk much more freely with James than I could with your mom, in many ways. It's been a very good thing."

David waited.

"And it might be a good thing for you, too," she said.

David stared at her without saying anything.

She said, "You could just meet with him for a minute when you give him the box of things your mom collected."

"I haven't found that yet."

"What's that?" she asked. David followed her gaze

over his shoulder to the kitchen table, where he'd left the box that had LAURA BOX written on the side. The folders were still spread out all over the table.

He said, "I mean, I want to go through it before I decide anything. It seems like a lot of junk. I don't really think it's anything this reporter needs."

"But your mom intended to pass it along. She must have thought it was important."

David said, "Why are you here?"

"What do you mean?"

"I mean, why are you here? Just to ask me to talk to the reporter again?"

"I came here to apologize."

"Really?"

"Yes."

"Okay, go for it."

"I did."

"Pretty sure at some point in an apology you're supposed to say 'I'm sorry.' You just talked about your therapy, told me some things you thought my mom would want, then bothered me about the very thing it is I think you thought you apologized for."

"You've misunderstood me."

"I understand you just fine, Becky. Look, I really have to finish packing."

He stood up. Becky stayed sitting, searching for some words. David walked to the door and she finally stood and followed him down the stairs. David walked back up the split level while she put on her shoes, got her jacket. She opened the door, then turned around. David was almost in the kitchen but stopped when she said, "I know this is your house now. But I've been coming here every week for twenty-five years. It's a second home to me, and to not feel welcome is a blow to me. I loved your mom, too. And I loved Laura. I know you don't like to talk about Laura and you get defensive. But I'm sorry, I had a relationship with Laura too. She was my best friend. Everything in my life happened because of Laura, and that isn't something you can smirk away from me or anyone else. The pain is shared by a lot of people — it's not your own thing that you get to keep. People cared about her and it's not your right to judge or to try to keep people away. You don't own Laura's story."

David said, "Is that another apology?"

Becky looked at him a long time, then closed the door and left.

CHAPTER FIFTEEN

DAVID PULLED THE COLD pizza from the night before out of the fridge. He ate a slice and looked over the living room. The house was halfway packed. He'd taken frames off the wall and leaned them. Unplugged some things. Made a pile of linens. A stack of unpacked boxes leaned against the wall. He thought it'd be easier to just sell the place and realized, a moment later, that he could do that.

When David had turned eighteen he'd gone to the bank with his mom and she'd set up the chequing account he still used. When he started full-time at Walmart, she'd asked if they did any matching contributions to RRSPs. David didn't know. He'd given her the employee booklet that had been given to him with the HR forms. She'd filled them out for him, and every month for the past twelve years, an amount had been deducted that ended up on his taxes each year. In April, he would give his mom his T4 and she would file his taxes through an accountant, who was an old family friend.

He thought he should start by seeing how much money his mom had. He went over to her computer and shook the mouse. A dialogue box told him the update had completed and asked him to click to restart. He packed while it booted up, and then cleared the pop-ups. He scanned down her bookmarks, which he now saw were links to the message boards and news articles she'd printed out. He eventually found her bank and was prompted for a password. He tried "pewtersocks," "Harold," "David," "Laura," and a few other likely ones. None of them worked. He opened the door that housed the computer tower and found a list of passwords taped to the back side. He typed in "nosrehpcm_49."

She had more in chequing than he would have thought, but there was no savings account. Her credit card had a few hundred on it for gas she'd bought the day before she died. David found a folder labelled "Accounting" on her desktop but couldn't make sense of the spreadsheet. Beside the password list on the drawer, he'd seen a phone number list. He plugged the rotary phone back in and called her accountant. Janet said,

"I've been trying to get in touch with you for weeks."

"The phone's been giving me trouble."

"No worries," she said. "And of course, I'm so sorry about your mom. I'm sorry I missed the funeral—I found out too late. She was such a good friend."

David said he knew, and was sorry she'd missed it.

"It would be good if you came in so I could walk you through a few things and tell you what's going on with the estate. I haven't heard from your mom's lawyer yet, but I believe I'm the executor of the estate. I mean, it's all left to you, but she thought you might need some help sorting through the financial end of things. Unless she changed the will from the last time we talked about it?"

David said, "Right. I'm not sure. I haven't talked to a lawyer yet. I didn't realize I should."

There was a pause on the other end of the line. Janet said, "Yes. You will need to talk to a lawyer. I think I've got the number around here."

David looked at the list and said, "I've got it."

"Great. Once you get in touch with them, I can walk you through everything. Your mom had RRSPs, GICs, and other investments. It's all going to be straight-forward since there's only you. But you'll need to bring the bank the death certificate, after you talk to the law-yer. Then we can look into transferring things into your name or cashing out or whatever you want. I'll walk you through it all, don't worry. But the lawyer is the first step."

David said thanks. Hung up. Dialed the other number.

The lawyer also said she'd been trying to get in touch with him since she'd read the obituary; she was sorry not to have made it to the funeral, but she'd seen the notice too late. "I've known your mother since I drew up the purchase agreement for your house, back in the seventies, I think it was. It was really just so hard to find out I missed the funeral. I'm so sorry."

Everything was very straightforward — she had worked on the will revision with his mom after his dad died and it was all going to David. He would have to come in and sign some things, and she mentioned probate and of course she had some fees, but it wouldn't amount to much. And the inheritance would be taxed, of course, but an accountant could explain all that. And the house, of course, was David's. She said it would not be taxed, as it was his place of residence, but if he sold it, it would be taxed unless he bought again right away, but those were all things David would have to discuss with his real estate agent. "Even if you don't want to sell, you'll have to get the place appraised for taxes, of course."

David said, "Of course. I will contact my real estate agent immediately."

They set up a time to meet later that week and David looked down the list for a real estate agent. There wasn't one.

All over town there were billboards that said "If you want it gone, call Jonny Shawn," with a picture of a youngish man in a loud shirt standing beside a "Sold" sign in front of a stately mansion. His website had that same stately mansion as a background. He stepped onto the screen and his mouth moved, then a dialog box popped up asking how he could help. David found his number at the bottom of the screen and called. A secretary asked for a few details — David explained he lived in the house, it was at the bottom of Mountain Road, and he'd just inherited it — and then asked when a good time for Mr. Shawn to call back would be. David said any time would be fine — if he didn't pick up, just try again, he didn't check messages. She laughed and said no one did these days. She thought Mr. Shawn would be back in an hour or so and would give him a call then.

He hung up the phone and it started ringing immediately. A real ring — a little metal hammer bouncing between two bells inside. David considered, waited for the fourth ring, and then picked it up. He said, "This is the McPherson residence, we're unable to come to the phone right now, please leave a message." He had planned to make the beep noise by pressing a number on the phone before he realized it was a rotary and he couldn't do that. He considered ways to make a beep noise but instead he waited. Eventually, his boss, Randy, said, "I don't think I heard a beep. David, it's Randy. We've got a couple of police officers here who wanted to talk to you about one of our customers, please give a call—"

David said, "Hey, Randy, what's going on?"

"Oh, you're there. It's about that Sanderson guy who roughed up the hooker. They're talking to Jamie right now and have some questions for you."

"I haven't been in to work in weeks. Why would they need to talk to me?"

"They didn't say. Could you come down here?"

"Sure. I'll be there in fifteen."

CHAPTER SIXTEEN

TWO POLICE CRUISERS WERE parked on the curb in front of the Walmart. David nodded to Norm, the greeter who he'd worked with for eight years. Norm said, "Welcome to Walmart. Can I help you find anything." David shook his head and walked toward the back.

Casey sat on a pallet under the mezzanine eating a chocolate bar. He said, "Jamie's talking to the cops."

"I know, that's why I'm here."

"Shit, you got to talk to them too?"

"I guess. Where's Randy?"

"He's up there too."

"Do they want to talk to you?"

"No, I don't know nothing."

"You can't eat those." David pointed at the open box

of chocolate bars beside Casey, meant for the candy section out front.

"The package was ripped."

"Randy has literally had employees charged by the police for eating damaged food."

"It doesn't matter, come on."

"I know it doesn't matter. I'm just saying. They take it very serious here."

"Whatever. Do you even work here anymore?"

David went up the stairs and knocked on Randy's door. At the same time, Jamie came out of the break room and said, "Oh shit, hey man."

"What's up?"

Two cops came out behind Jamie. Randy opened the door to his office. David stepped back so Randy could come out. The mezzanine felt crowded. David, taller than both cops, felt small. One said, "Are you the guy?"

"David McPherson. Randy said you wanted to talk to me?"

The second cop opened his notepad. He said, "You're the garden section manager?"

"That's right.

Randy added, "You asked me to call in the shift manager from the day Jamie sold the items to your suspect."

"Come with us, please."

David followed them into the break room.

. . .

THE POLICE CAME TO their house a few hours after Laura's Discman had been found on the mountain. David watched two cars pull into the driveway: a marked police car and a sedan. Two men in suits got out of the sedan, two uniformed officers out of the squad car. David's mom had come up to the window without him noticing. She said, "Oh God no, no no," when she saw the suits.

David's aunt had gone down to open the door but his mom rushed down to the split level and asked, "Did you find her?"

"No. But could we come in a minute?"

They asked to speak privately with David's parents. The two plainclothes officers followed David's mom and dad into the dining room. The two uniformed officers stood in the kitchen with his aunt. She offered them a coffee or tea. One said no thank you, the other yes, which led the first to reconsider and say he might as well. Their leather belts creaked; the pouches and pockets clicked. They both sat at the table, taking up more space than they should. The younger of the two officers saw David looking and nodded.

He went up to his room and tried to read until his mom called him down.

Her eyes were red. She said the police had found

Laura's Discman and thought she might be somewhere on the mountain. They wanted to ask David a few questions.

They took him into the dining room. The room only used for holiday meals. All dark wood and old furniture. Always cold; the heat was never turned on in there. A drink side cart. Framed photos of long-dead relatives in black and white. A taxidermized deer head.

The two police came in with him. His mom said, "I'll be right here," and stood by the door. One of the detectives opened his notebook. The other offered David a chair and pulled out one for himself. They were on the same side of the table, but not sitting at it. The space between them was close. The officer leaned forward and smiled. He said, "We've got a few questions for you, son, if you don't mind."

David felt like everyone suddenly thought he was eight. He said, "Sure."

"WE'VE JUST GOT A couple of questions," the first cop said. David sat down at the break table.

"Sure, yeah. Go for it."

"Do you recognize this man?"

The police put a photo down in front of him. David said, "Yeah, that's the Sanderson guy."

The other officer took a note. The first said, "So you know him."

"No."

"But you said you know him."

David felt a blush creeping up, which got worse when he thought it might make him seem suspicious, but even if he seemed suspicious it didn't matter, he told himself, because he didn't know anything. He said, "No, I know who he is."

"But you don't know him?"

"His picture was on the news." David wished he had explained that first. He was confused.

"Right. But you've sold things to him here?"

"I don't think so."

"Your colleague, Jamie, said so."

"A lot of people come in here. I don't remember all of them."

The two cops looked at each other. The one who had been taking notes stepped back and took a laptop off the kitchen counter. He put it on the table and clicked, turned it to face David. David recognized the garden section; it was security footage. David saw himself talking to Jamie. Then walking down the aisle. The quality of the footage was surprisingly good; they had upgraded to HD cameras a year before. David could clearly see himself approaching a customer, smiling and waving. He wouldn't have recognized it was Sanderson if the Lucky Lager hat had not been so prominent.

The cop paused the video.

"You seem to be pretty friendly with him."

David said, "I mean, we are supposed to be friendly to customers. Three-metre rule."

"What's that."

"It's how we're supposed to engage customers." David pointed to the break room floor. A decal had been laid down. Written on the wall above was "Remember the Three-Metre Rule." The decal had three metres marked off. At the third metre it said "Eye contact"; at the second "Smile"; and at the first "Can I help you?" Every time you came into or left the break room, you were reminded of it.

"You do this with every customer?"

"Between you and me, only if it can't be avoided."

The second cop laughed and some of the tension left David.

The first said, "But you sold him some stuff?"

"I don't work the tills."

He held out a paper to David. It was a receipt for twenty feet of chain and several bags of soil. David's employee code was in the top right corner. David got nervous again. He said, "I really can't remember…"

"You said you don't work the till?"

"Sometimes I'll ring a thing in at the back desk if

I helped someone, but I don't remember this." They stared at him. He said, "There's cameras on all the tills. If I sold it to him, you guys would know, wouldn't you?"

"Any reason anyone would want to log in as you?"

"None that I can think of. I mean, the log-in code is just our initials. People accidentally log in as someone else all the time."

The first cop looked back at the second. He nodded slightly. The first said, "That's all we need from you. If anything else about this comes to mind, let us know?"

David left the room. The sweat, now free of the stifling room, cooled under his arms. He raised them both and flapped them and then realized the cops were coming out after him. He stepped forward and Randy came out of his office and it was again crowded.

"Constables," Randy said. "Did you get everything you need?"

"Could we have a word with you?"

"Of course. David, I'd like to talk with you after I'm done. Could you stick around." He looked at the cops. "A few minutes?"

The second cop shrugged. David said, "I'll grab a coffee and be back in a bit."

He found Jamie under the mezzanine with Casey. "Get a coffee with me?"

"Sure thing," Jamie said.

Casey followed them out and David realized he was going to come to the coffee place. He said, "Oh, Casey, I almost forgot. Randy wants you to move the shopping carts. The cops have them blocked in, so could you move them to the other side of the door, then do a parking lot sweep?"

"Ah, shit man."

"Sorry."

Jamie and David went to the Tim Hortons across the parking lot. He told Jamie to get a seat and he stood in line for the coffee. He waited. Looked at the photos of the owner of the franchise holding the Stanley Cup over his head; the second-best player of all time was slapping him on the back. There was another photo beside that of the same guy facing off against the greatest player of all time. The owner's name was Trent Blake. He'd grown up in Griffiths and moved back after his career ended. He hadn't been very a good player. He'd been traded around a lot and was one of those bag-of-pucks-thrown-in parts of a bigger deal that put him on the Cup-winning team. He'd only been called up to the final to fill in for injuries, but that was enough to get his name on the Cup. He ended up finishing his career in Vancouver, which was big news locally. He'd gotten into the Tim Hortons franchises after he retired. They liked to give them to old hockey players to keep the brand going. He'd been in some trouble recently because he slept with the doughnut girls and he was their boss and they were teenagers.

David put a coffee in front of Jamie and sat down. He said, "Are you okay?"

"Better, yeah. What was that all about?"

"What did they ask you?"

"About the Sanderson guy. They thought I was trying to hide something. They had footage of me selling him all the shit he used on the girl and tried to say I was trying to hide it because I used your log-in."

"On purpose?"

Jamie looked up at him, then down at his coffee. "Yeah man. Sorry. I log in all the time as different names."

"Why?"

"I don't know. They track everything there, you know? Like you punch in. Then they look at customer interactions. They see how much you go to the till. I just, I sometimes do things to fuck around with the numbers. You know. Screw up their data a little. Sorry."

David shook his head. "You tell them that?"

"No, I just said I must have hit the wrong keys. But they could tell something was up. I mean, the *J* and the *D* are pretty far from each other, I guess. But if I told them they'd tell Randy and I can't get fired, you know. It's stupid. I'm sorry. Did they give you a hard time?"

"I think they were just checking their boxes. They found something suspicious and needed to see what was up. I told them people logged in accidentally as other people. I'm sure it's fine. Randy will probably give you a lecture about making sure to log in as yourself or something. And you should stop doing that."

He said, "I will. Fuck. I'm sorry."

Jamie rubbed his eyes, then looked out the window at the parking lot. David said, "When I started on the floor Randy used to work with me on my shifts all the time. He'd call me up into his office once a week and go through any mistake I made on the till. Like, if I punched in that it was a Mastercard transaction when it was Visa or shit like that. It was obviously a mistake and I never meant to, but every week we'd sit there and he'd work his way through a pile of receipts with everyone. So, whenever he was on the floor with me and would go to the till, I'd get the next customer, log in as him, and punch in the information wrong."

Jamie said, "No way."

"I liked the idea of him setting up a mirror and lecturing himself about getting it right."

"That's amazing."

"A few months later they installed the cameras on the till and I'm almost positive it wasn't because they were worried about theft, but because Randy started to think something was up and wanted to catch whoever it was. So really, don't worry about it. I get it. But do stop. Anyways, you good? With the cops and stuff?"

"Yeah man, thanks."

They picked up their coffees and went outside. Casey was pushing a line of shopping carts toward the store. David said, "I got to head off."

"I thought you were going to talk to Randy?"

"I'd prefer not to."

"Are you quitting?"

"I don't know."

"What should I tell Randy?"

"Say I got a call and needed to skip out but I said I'll get in touch later."

"I hope you come back, man. This place sucks without you."

"I promise you it sucks just as much with me there."

David slapped Jamie's shoulder and walked away.

CHAPTER SEVENTEEN

DAVID CALLED CAROLYN WHEN he got home. He said to her voice mail, "Hey, it's David McPherson, Laura's brother," which he immediately regretted and tried to change, but could not access the voice mail menu to restart it with a rotary phone. He went on, "Sorry, that was a stupid start and I'm on my mom's old phone so those clicks you maybe heard were me trying to erase it on a rotary phone. Anyways, I'm stuck with it. So...
I guess give me a call?"

He put the phone down. It started ringing. He hoped Carolyn was like everyone else and didn't bother to check voice mail. He picked it up.

"You want it gone?"

David said, "What?"

"You want it gone? This is Jonny Shawn. 'If you want it gone, call Jonny Shawn.'"

"Right. I'm not sure if I 'want it gone' but I just inherited a house that's way too big for me and should probably downsize, so I'm looking at options."

He said, "Sure sure sure, absolutely," and asked David about the location, which he said was "hot."

"Big development up the mountain, big park nearby, and more people than ever are commuting to Nanaimo and the mainland. The island is becoming the Brooklyn of Vancouver," he said. "I'm booked up tomorrow but could stop by Friday morning and take a look? We can go over options then."

David started organizing the house so it would be presentable for Jonny Shawn. He closed boxes and stacked them. He gave the kitchen a sweep and then repacked the files from the Laura box. The VHS tape was last. He slipped it out and read the note again. *I hope this can bring you some comfort.*

David's mom had a shelf of videos from when he was young. Mostly Disney movies in oversized plastic cases, but also some comedies he'd liked—early Sandler, Farley, pretty much anything starring the nineties cast of *SNL*. She never watched any of them anymore, but had held on to her VHS player in case, one day, she might. She'd made David, ten years before, make sure it was wired into the then-new DVD player and satellite box.

David put the tape from his sister's box into the player and pressed Play. He then gathered up all the remotes he could find and took a few minutes to figure out which combination of power buttons, inputs, and channels would make the VHS appear on screen. An in-progress news report came on, his sister's face, in cap and gown, on screen. He pressed Rewind and started again from the beginning. The screen was blank for a minute, and then the old anchor from the Victoria news appeared on screen. He said, "Tonight, a young woman missing in a small town an hour north of Victoria..."

THE FIRST REPORTERS ARRIVED the day after David's sister went missing. His mom and dad were working their way through their address book, calling people, letting them know, asking them to call if they heard anything at all. Becky and the yearbook committee had shown up that morning. They had made a missing poster and were handing out flyers all over town. David's aunt cooked, made coffee, put food in front of them, as she'd do for the next three weeks.

David went into the living room and turned on the TV. The noon news started, and his sister's photo came on the screen. His uncle sat down beside him and said, "It's not time for such distractions." He stared at David until he got up and turned off the TV. "It's important," the uncle said, "for the family to be together now."

An hour later, David was sitting on the couch looking at the road when a van with the local news logo on the side pulled up. The adults discussed what to do. His mom and dad had been awake all night and didn't feel up to talking. David's uncle said he could do it. David watched, from the big bay window, his uncle get interviewed. The bright light on his face, the reporter standing beside his cameraman, holding a mic between them. He wasn't out there long—Laura was only missing then; there wasn't much to say.

There was nothing to do the next morning, so David got his laundry together, went down the split level, and started a load. He sat on the washing machine for a minute and then opened the door to the rest of the basement. His dad had only ever got as far as framing off the rooms down there; the in-house garage never had a car in it, so there was no point in blocking it off from the rest of the basement. There were boxes, Christmas decorations, stacks of chairs, baby clothes. Basement stuff. David found their old TV in a wood cabinet with upholstered speakers on either side. With the bunny ears, he could get the channel out of Victoria.

Each morning, David would walk downstairs with a laundry hamper, then sneak through the door and turn on the TV. He kept the volume low so he could hear through the vent if his absence had been noticed, and he put in an appearance every hour or so — walking by with the hamper or some other busy work. After Laura's Discman was found and the search started, he didn't have to be as careful. He would run a tray of muffins or coffee urn out for the searchers first thing in the morning, then sneak around to the basement door and watch TV or read comics. He moved an old armchair in front of the TV. He used a box as a side table. Every couple of hours, he went outside, found an empty tray, and brought it to the kitchen. It stuck in people's minds that he was helping. Until they found Laura's body, the basement was his private little space.

He watched the game shows in the morning. The talk shows in the afternoon. Sitcoms at night. Broken up, every few hours, by the news. Which was the only place he heard what was going on with Laura.

DAVID WATCHED THE OLD footage. A shot of the town. Becky hanging up a poster with Laura's face on it. And his uncle saying, "We're all praying for her safe return." A picture of Laura in her school tracksuit came up on screen; this was before the grad photo was used. Anyone with information was asked to call. The clip ended. Another started.

The clips were just the segments related to Laura, not the whole newscast. But whoever copied the tapes included every broadcast from each day—the morning, noon, six o'clock, and evening news. A different anchor would set up the story, but, early on, the same story would re-air. After two and a half days' worth of the same reports, the 11 p.m. newscast started with the anchor saying, "Police have found a lead in the disappearance of a girl missing an hour north of Victoria." The Discman had been found; Laura was the top story.

The segments were longer after that. Each day had fresh footage, but all showed the same things. Shots of searchers congregating in David's front yard. A helicopter flying down the Robertson River. Interviews with searchers, saying they were just doing what anyone else would do, they were there to help, if it was their own daughter. His uncle blessing the volunteers. Footage of outside the house, tents set up. Searchers in small groups, getting their assignments for the day. Going over maps spread out on card tables. Men loading into work crummies donated by the logging companies. Police talking into radios. His aunt bustling out of the house with trays of baked goods. He remembered each newscast, even as they blurred into sameness.

The "Breaking News" banner graphic caught David off guard. The anchor said, "A tragic end to the search for..."

A crowd gathered around the edge of a clear-cut. An image of police tape uselessly strung around few trees. A cut to an ambulance coming down the mountain road outside David's house, and then David's dad, held up by searchers, walking out of the woods. The anchor narrated that the body of Laura McPherson, a girl missing in Griffiths, BC, had been found. The death was deemed suspicious; the police would be giving a full report at nine the next morning. David's uncle asked everyone to pray for Laura. Said she was in a better place.

The next day, a person of interest being questioned. His uncle again, saying that at least they had closure. Further requests for leads. More of the same, more of the same. And the funeral. The camera crews not allowed in. The overflowed church parking lot. Pictures of "Closed for Funeral" signs on local businesses. The line of cars following the hearse. And then occasional updates, asks for leads. The news set changed, the anchor a year older, and then a new one in the next clip. And then the screen went black.

Just as David was about to stop the tape, his uncle appeared on screen again. He said, "Right here is good?" and a reporter off camera responded, "Maybe get you under the awning so there's less shadow," and the whole rig moved. And then the questions that weren't heard in the news clips David had watched earlier: How does the family feel? When was she last seen? Did she have a history of this? Any statement? It was the last question, which his uncle answered as a combination of the three previous, that led to the quote used in the newscast. And then the reporter thanked him, David's uncle nodded and turned toward the house, and the screen went blank as he reached out for the doorknob.

A second clip started. Downtown Griffiths, outside of the high school as it appeared twenty years ago. Cars drove by. They looked ancient. Small lowered pickup trucks and IROC-ZS that had been popular when David was in school but which he hadn't seen or thought about in years. The parent cars, boxier than he remembered. The camera panned across the front of the school to the running track. The sign had been changed to "Go Turds." A group of kids walked by the camera. They looked familiar but weren't clear enough to make out until Chad Doskel faced the camera, spread his legs, and hit both his hips. David remembered that the gesture had been popular at the time—it meant "suck it." Another thing he hadn't thought about in years. The clip ended.

Another started. This was the sign outside of town, on the highway, that welcomed people to Griffiths. David realized he was watching the raw footage that had been edited into the news segments. Five minutes of filming, cut down into ten seconds. Full interviews with his uncle, the police, searchers. Establishing shots of the town, the house, the mountain.

Another clip of an older woman, looking closely at the missing poster, filmed from across the street. And then Becky and the other girls taking posters out of the box. The camera zoomed in close, its small movements blurring the scene. When the zoom stopped, the camera focused on Becky's thong, which came up above her jeans. The angle blurred, then focused in on where Robyn Millard's shirt had tugged down enough to see her breast as far as her black bra. She looked at the camera and the clip ended.

The search started. Not edited into action, the clips were dull and static, none of it seeming as urgent as it appeared on the news. A five-minute clip of people milling around the front yard, drinking coffee. They point up, a cop comes. He says something not caught by the camera. A couple of them laugh. The sounds all distant. Birds chirping closer to the camera picked up clearly. Tires crunching gravel. A truck pulls up in front of the camera and the searchers get in and head up the mountain.

There were dozens of similar scenes. Mr. Murray talking to his uncle while getting coffee. The high-school gym teacher in a reflector vest, looking lost without a group of kids to boss around. Mr. Davies, David's alcoholic grade-eight social studies teacher, talking to the middle-school principal. Jay, who's name wasn't Jay but who had run a store called Jay's

Handimart, accepting a muffin from his aunt. All slapping their arms and blowing steam in the cold morning air. It drizzled in some shots and was grey in the early morning. Dogs were handled. In one clip, David could barely make himself out in the ground-level window in the basement, watching.

Shots of searchers walking through the woods, work trucks driving by with loads of people. A long shot of the gate at the entrance to the logging road; nothing happening, just the gate and swaying trees. A clip of an ambulance parked on the roadside surrounded by searchers and police. The camera panned to a clear-cut where a few people walked toward the camera, picking their way slowly across the stumps and slash. David realized they were carrying his sister's body on a stretcher.

He paused the tape.

Unpaused.

The news station must have heard about the discovery of the body on the CB radios everyone used during the search. They had set up on the logging road, looking across the clear-cut to where the searchers came out of the woods. As they got closer to the camera, David made out police, paramedics, and search-and-rescue. They struggled to lift the gurney with Laura's tarp-covered body over the slash. Mr. Murray was with them; David hadn't known that. It was only when the gurney had made it most of the way across the clearing, five minutes into the footage, that the camera swung around to a van that was pulling in. David's dad had arrived on the scene. He got out of the van and the camera followed him as he walked toward the searchers. A police officer and Mr. Murray stopped him halfway. They talked. Mr. Murray put his hand on David's dad's shoulder. David's dad nodded a couple of times and then they walked toward the gurney. The other searchers gave him space. He didn't try to look under the tarp. Just placed a hand on it. He said something and everyone gathered around the sides and lifted with him. This was where the clip used in the newscast started. Somewhere to the side of the video camera, the newspaper photographer took the photo that won the awards and which David always saw. Here, the angles were different, the whole scene filmed. David had always thought, as had everyone, that his dad had been in the search party that found the body.

He watched interviews with searchers—all of them devastated, they said, that it had ended this way. And then shots of the crowd going into the funeral. Coming out. They had requested the media stay away from the burial, so the following clip was of the house. The cameraman seemed to be trying to get lighting shots. A short clip in one spot, another clip elsewhere, across the street. The empty tents set up, food coming out, awaiting everyone arriving after the burial. Shots of cars rolling in, parking all the way up Mountain Road and then all the way down Sherman Road. People greeted by family. David saw himself in a too-large suit. He went to the front door. A long shot of some of his sister's friends getting out of a car. Their mom followed. The camera zoomed in on the mom's chest and followed them to the reception.

David's dad shook hands. A line of people hugging. A time jump. The whole house on screen to catch the size of the crowd, overflowing from the driveway to the street. A couple minutes in the camera zoomed and started to pan across. It took David a few seconds to realize the camera was zooming in on a girl, and then a few more to recognize her. Staci Greene, who had been banned from their house for whippits. She wore a black high-neck button-up dress and black tights that were actually thigh-high boots. You could see this because her skirt was short and when she walked a bit of skin where her butt and thigh met was visible. The camera zoomed in close as she walked down the driveway and away from the house. She had a book in her hand. The camera stayed tight on her legs and butt. She stepped behind a car, the camera zoomed out, and Staci got into the passenger side of a beige Camaro with a black driver's-side door. The screen went black and there was no further footage.

David rewound and paused at Staci getting into the

Camaro. He recognized it because of the door, which was obviously a replacement. In grade ten he and his friend had started going to the pool hall near the school. It had been a biker hangout in the seventies, but by the mid-nineties business was not great, and they'd brought in arcades to bring school kids over. David and his friends went there to play Road Rage and a couple of other arcade games; they avoided the pool area because of the older guys, but would stand out front to get fresh air and drink Jones sodas. David had been leaning on the Camaro one day and the owner came out and grabbed David by the shirt. He told David not to touch his fucking car ever again. He held his finger in David's face for a long time before he let him down. He went back in. David's friend Eric said, "Holy shit," and Mark, the tougher of them, said, "The car is a piece of shit anyways." David laughed uncomfortably and then the guy came back out. He slammed David into the wall twice. He said, "You never, never fucking laugh at me again. You understand?"

They didn't go to the pool hall after that, but David had seen the guy's car parked there almost every day all through high school; he learned later his name was Ranger and he apparently sold drugs, but never to anyone at the school that David knew. Once, at a party right after he graduated, David had run into him — literally. Walked into him, drunk, in a hallway. David had frozen up, but Ranger hadn't recognized him because it had been years and the incident, to him, was nothing. He just said, "Watch where you're going, bud," and tapped David's beer bottle with his.

David rewound to the start of the crowd shot. Thirty seconds in, Staci came out of the house. She made it halfway across the lawn before the cameraman saw her. He zoomed in. She had a book in her hand. She got into the Camaro. David rewound again. She came out of the house. She kept the book pressed to one side, away from the crowd, while she walked down the driveway.

David rewound further. He found a clip where his mom was hugging people and you could see Staci walking by in the background. She was only visible for two seconds, walking toward the house. He tried to pause. It was blurry but he was sure she wasn't carrying anything. He fast-forwarded to her leaving the house with a book.

He paused the recording again and went up the stairs to Laura's room. Everything was in its place. He opened her desk drawer. There were pens, scissors, notepads. Her school stuff. He found a diary and flipped through. It went up to a few days before she went missing. It wasn't really a diary. More of a weekly planner with her notes about what she'd done and who she saw. At the beginning of each week there were goals. Things like *finish science project*, *get yearbook proofs in*, but also *see the Brakofs, be kinder to David.* At the end of the week, a quick reflection. There was nothing interesting there, but then of course there wouldn't be. The police had looked through all of her stuff at the time.

He heard the phone downstairs ringing and turned to see the gears in Laura's phone trying to move. David stared at it a minute before picking it up.

"Hey, it's Carolyn. Carolyn Murray. I used to live across the street," she said.

"I was hoping you wouldn't listen to the message."

"It was funny. I'm in town picking up some more paperwork. Can I stop by?"

"Sure, I actually have something I want to ask you about."

"That's mysterious."

"It's probably nothing. Just found something weird in my sister's stuff."

"I'll be by in fifteen."

CHAPTER EIGHTEEN

WHEN CAROLYN SAW THE living room she said, "Jesus. This hasn't changed much, has it?"

"You should see Laura's room."

"Oh, no. The same?"

"I knew Mom didn't touch it right after Laura died, but I thought by now she might have. It's pretty fucked."

She looked around again and said, "This is weird. It takes me right back. I feel like it even smells the same."

"I've actually been trying to fix that." David showed her a box of plug-in air fresheners he'd taken out.

Carolyn picked up one and smelled. "There it is."

"We live at the edge of hundreds of miles of forest and my mom wants the house to smell like Pine

Wonderland. You want one? They discontinued this scent a few years ago, so my mom had me order two boxes off the internet. There's several dozen left, if you're interested."

"Hard pass, thanks." She said, "It's so different all around here. Like, the road is the same, but I don't know any of those houses. I couldn't even figure out where mine is."

"It got torn down. Someone bought it and completely razed the land. Trees, grass, house, everything. Started over. There's three houses there now."

"That explains it."

"But the rock is still there. The one with your address on it." David pointed out the rock through the big window. She didn't remember a rock.

She said, "So, you had something you wanted to talk to me about."

"Right. Do you have any idea why Staci Greene would have come to my sister's funeral?"

"I don't remember her being there."

"Me neither. But I was watching this old news footage someone sent my mom. In one of the clips of the funeral you can see Staci Greene in the crowd and she goes into the house. Later, she comes out with a book and gets into a Camaro that belonged to some sketchy dude who used to hang out at the pool hall. I think his name was Ranger."

NOT THAT KIND OF PLACE

"Can I see?"

David started the tape and rewound it. He said, "The cameraman seems to have been a pervert. The only reason I knew it was Staci was because he zooms in on her ass."

"Really?"

"Watch." He started the clip at the crowd shot.

She said, "Wow. We're all there."

"Yeah."

David watched Carolyn watch. She seemed to be holding down tears, until the camera started zooming in on Staci. She said, "You weren't kidding."

"There's a real good shot of Mrs. Mays's tits in another clip."

"Jesus." She looked at the screen. "Can I watch that again?"

David rewound. He showed her Staci in the crowd, then coming out of the house with something. And then paused when she got into the Camaro. He said, "Ranger threatened to kill me for leaning on his car. I think he sold drugs or something. He was always at the pool hall, at least."

Carolyn said, "What are you thinking?"

"Well, it's just weird, isn't it? Like, why was Staci even here? She and my sister hadn't been friends in years."

"They were still friends."

"Were they?"

199

"Yeah. After the whippit thing, your sister would say she was working on a project or going to the library or something and then go hang out with Staci."

"I'm shocked my sister lied to my parents. She was such a rule follower."

"To a point. But if she thought a rule was stupid, she would break it. Your mom banned Staci by association—not because she'd done anything—so your sister ignored it."

"I had no idea."

Carolyn looked at the screen. David had paused it at the end of the clip. The lines of tape static distorted the image. She said, "If Ranger sold drugs he was probably friends with Brandon. Staci was living with him, and he had her working for him too."

"Staci sold drugs?"

Carolyn looked at David.

He said, "Oh. Sex work."

"Yeah, there were a few girls from the school who went down to Fuller's Bay for 'parties.'"

He said, "Wait, she would have been, like, sixteen."

"Yeah."

"I guess I should stop being surprised about things like that."

"People can be very sheltered from what's going on all around them. I only knew because your sister told me about Staci. By grade twelve Staci had pretty much dropped out and I didn't see much of her. I was much more...Christian about things back then."

"You weren't friends with her?"

"Like I said, I was only really friends with Laura. But Laura was loyal to anyone she had ever been friends with. It's why she could still be friends with a dorky 'Christian Camp girl,' even though I'd long been labelled a social liability."

"It's weird, I always thought you guys were all friends with each other."

"Not at all. Laura and I had been inseparable in elementary school. We walked to the bus stop together, sat together on the bus and beside each other in class, hung out after school. And then, in middle school, all of the sudden we went from being around the same twenty kids we'd seen every day for six years to being in a school with a hundred new kids who were just starting to have their hormones kick into overdrive. And everyone went crazy, and all of the sudden people were being awful to each other. It hadn't really occurred to me I was anything but a kid until then," Carolyn said. "Everyone in elementary school knew I was just a quiet kid who went to church, but then in middle school, it was suddenly something I had to explain and justify."

"Believe it or not," David said, "I was a dweeb in elementary school too. But, yeah, it was fine. Everyone knew me and Eric and Brian didn't like sports and liked to play Dr.-Who-Meets-Star-Trek at lunch hour. But in the first week of grade seven, we went behind the middle school to play make-believe. There was a grade nine rugby practice just starting and, consequently, we stuck to the library after that day."

"Exactly," Carolyn said. "I could have done with a few more years of Barbies and Disney movies, but I learned pretty quick it was *YM* and *Tiger Beat* time. Which created a problem with my parents. They wouldn't let me have that stuff, and that outed me as a dork. And I took Laura down by association. But Laura didn't care about any of that stuff, like I said. She never bought into that, or even seemed to notice or care about it. Even though we hung out a lot less after the whippit thing—my parents started making me go to youth group in Chemainus, and Laura start doing after-school sports and stuff, so we never saw each other—we were still friends."

Carolyn looked at the screen again. She said, "Staci was pretty much the same thing. They were kind of friendly after that project they worked on, but what really made them close was me and Laura getting in trouble with a group of stoners Staci knew. I have no idea why they chose us, but they called us dykes and made fun of us for being Christian or whatever. We didn't understand it. We'd done nothing. And I, at least, had no idea what a dyke was. I actually remember looking it up in the library and being even more confused.

I was like, 'how?' But anyways, these girls were relentless. They'd like write 'sluts' on our locker and heckle us in the halls.

"Staci told them to lay off and they didn't and one day while we were waiting for the bus one of them came over and said something about us sucking the priest's cock and Staci jumped her. Like, pushed her over, straddled her chest, and punched her in the head until a teacher separated them. She got suspended and, after that, Laura and her were friends for life. I think it was right after that that we went to the party, and there was no way Laura would listen to your mom about not seeing Staci."

"I had no idea my sister got bullied. I always kind of thought of her as on the side of the bullies, you know?"

"It's different for a brother. And your sister hung out with everyone, so there were some jerks."

"Trevor called me a faggot all the time at school, and then all of the sudden they were dating and he was all nice to me. Like 'just kidding about all that, bud.' And then any time I'd see him after him and Becky got together he acted like we were old friends."

"Wait, Becky and him got together?"

"You didn't know?"

"I left, remember?"

"They have three kids. They broke up. He had a second family in Alberta by a teenager."

"Oh God. Poor Becky."

"I mean, I guess, but she was just as bad as him — she would come over and make jokes about me and Eric being bum buddies or whatever shit kids said back then — and she's even worse now. She's been hounding me to see this reporter, and seems indignant that I a) don't want to, and b) don't like her at all."

"Well, she was not great at self-reflection, even back in high school. I didn't like her at all, and I'm not even sure your sister did. Like, she was friends with Becky because she was friends with everyone, but it was more because they were in the same clubs that they hung out, I think."

"That makes . . . a lot of sense. I always thought it was kind of fucked that Becky anointed herself the 'mourning friend.'"

"I don't doubt she was hurt by it."

"I know. It's just... Everything she does is such a production."

They looked back at the screen. Staci's butt, the book in her hand, Ranger's Camaro. David said, "So I guess this is nothing."

"I don't know. Grabbing a book without asking is weird."

"Right?"

"Can you see what's on the cover?"

They watched the clip again. David said, "It didn't

really look like a *book* book, you know? I thought it was maybe a notebook or a diary. I looked in her room and found a diary in her desk. So it wasn't that."

Carolyn thought for a minute. She said, "Can we go up there? I just had a thought."

"Sure. But just to warn you, it's weird."

CHAPTER NINETEEN

DAVID PUSHED THE DOOR open and stepped out of the way. Carolyn went in. "You weren't kidding."

"Want to have a game of Girl Talk?" He pulled the box off Laura's game shelf.

"Oh my God." She took the box from him and read the back. David sat on the edge of Laura's bed. The springs creaked. Carolyn turned away.

David pulled a copy of *The Doctor's Book of Home Remedies* off the shelf and flipped through. Laura went through a hypochondriac phase a few years before she died. She would get a cold or a sore knee and look through a medical dictionary and diagnose herself with something or other. Their mom never took it seriously, so Laura would consult the home remedy guide and

give herself a treatment and then think she'd cured
herself of whooping cough or brain fever or whatever
she thought she had.

Carolyn said, "What are you going to do with all
this?"

"I've been thinking of burning the house down and
claiming the insurance money."

"So you won't mind if I take this?" She pointed at a
picture on the wall. It was Laura and Carolyn, probably in middle school. They wore coveralls with paint
all over them and were making a banner. "It was for a
youth group thing," Carolyn explained. "Laura would
come sometimes in middle school. She stopped when
she got busy with her sports..."

She turned away again.

David said, "Anything else you need? Ballet shoes?
Twenty-five-year-old scented candle? See-through
phone?"

She sniffled once and laughed. "I had one of those."

"It still works." On cue, the gears started spinning.
He added, "Sort of," and pulled the cord out of the wall.
It went dead, but he could hear the rotary phone ring-
ing downstairs.

Carolyn said, "The diary."

"Right." David opened the desk and pulled it out.
"It's just dates and stuff. Nothing interesting."

Carolyn crouched down by the bed and reached

under. Felt along the bottom and then lay down. She said, "Laura and I used to hide diaries from our parents to keep them from snooping. We would leave a 'safe' diary out for them to find and hide the real one in the box spring." She moved around. "There's a hole, but I can't find a book."

David pulled the mattress off the bed and tilted the box spring up so Carolyn could check.

Laura had made a slight cut right where the fabric stapled to the wooden frame. A few books were wedged between the spring and the frame. Carolyn worked them out and then David put the box spring back down and pulled the mattress on. They sat beside each other. Carolyn held the books on her lap. There were six.

"So," David said, "this is weird."

Carolyn said, "We started this in grade seven, after the whippits. My mom looked at my diary, which at the time had nothing at all in it except that I had a crush on James Talbot, who was in grade eight, and I worried that might hurt my chances with Jonathan Taylor Thomas."

"The kid from *Home Improvement*?"

"The very same. Anyways, I was mad at my mom, and Laura was worried your mom would look at hers, so we came up with this. I stopped in grade ten. My mom got me a new bed while I was away at summer

209

camp, and the old bedframe got thrown into the dump. She did not understand why I was crying about a new bedframe. I guess Laura kept it going."

Carolyn flipped open the first book. Laura had always been organized; she'd written the dates the diary covered on the front endpaper of each book when she completed it. The first four books covered middle school, the last two covered high school. Grade ten in one book, and eleven and twelve in the other. She said, "The last entry is March 12."

"And she died in May.

"So, one is missing?"

"I guess so."

"Why would Staci take one?"

"I mean, we don't know for sure she took it. Maybe the police found one? They searched in here a bunch. Or maybe Laura didn't start a new one?"

"Sure. But maybe she did."

David tapped the books. Sighed.

Carolyn said, "We should probably read some of it, huh?"

"I guess."

"Let's go downstairs. It's weird in here."

CAROLYN PUT THE BOOKS on the kitchen table and David made them coffee to put things off a few more minutes. The image of Staci was still paused on the screen. Carolyn sat down at the table and read the side of the box there. She said, "What's this?"

"My mom seems to have spent a lot of time reading unsolved mystery forums about Laura." David took the first file out. "'Island murder, possible family connection? New theory.'" He handed her the file.

"Oh, wow."

"Yeah. It seems kind of sad. It's all mostly nonsense. Even the theories that seem plausible are ruined by the company they keep. Like, it's all just people cobbling together stories, killing time. Do you remember Farley Moore?"

"The alien guy?"

"Yeah. There's a theory in there that Laura got picked up by aliens like Farley had, because Farley said he was going up the mountain to meet them and then disappeared."

"I remember that story. Farley, I mean. He said he was in contact with them for years."

"Local legend. They found pieces of his truck up by Pole Hill a couple of years ago. He blew himself up with dynamite, either because he was trying to launch his truck into space or because he wanted to blow himself up with dynamite. No one is sure. But no body, so some people still think the aliens got him."

"Jesus. Did your mom buy any of it?"

"I'd like to think she had the good sense not to believe that Laura is in space. But the other stuff? I don't know. I mean, there's so much of it. She must have thought someone was on to something."

He poured their coffees. "I have neither milk nor sugar."

"Black is fine."

They sat across from each other.

"I suppose we should start looking," Carolyn said.

"Yup." Neither moved. David laughed, then Carolyn. He said, "Fuck it," and opened the diary from grades eleven and twelve.

David flipped through the grade eleven stuff quickly to get to the beginning of grade twelve. He scanned an entry about the first day of school, another about missing Jonathan, who Laura dated before Trevor. He was a year older and had moved to Vancouver for school. They were trying to stay together, but Laura doubted it would work. Still, he was her "first love." David moved on. There was nothing interesting in the first month and the diary entries were weekly and sometimes short. "I should write in this more," she wrote, "but I feel like I just say the same things."

He flipped. Saw Staci's name. He said to Carolyn, "So, here's something about Staci. Apparently she hadn't been to school that year and Laura was worried. This is in October."

Carolyn thought about that. "I think I remember. I had been away at this Christian Camp thing all summer. And Laura worked a lot that summer, I think?"

"At the Burger King. She wanted to save money for her own car when she went to university."

"Right, so when school started we were all catching up on everything and I guess Laura didn't realize Staci wasn't there right away. I mean, she wasn't in any of our direct friend groups, and she skipped a lot and hung out in the park. They had way different interests. I think Laura had tried to get her on the basketball team when they got to high school, but she quit. Like, she wasn't someone we saw a lot. I do remember going to look for her at some point. I don't know, this was all so long ago."

David flipped through, found another mention. "Yeah, here it says you guys went to her mom's house." She'd lived in King Arthur's Court—an apartment block that had since been razed but was then a couch-on-the-lawn, loud-fights-out-front kind of place. "Looks like Staci's mom told you guys she hadn't seen Staci all summer and didn't fucking care where she was."

"Staci's home life," Carolyn said, "was not great."

Laura wrote that she had asked a group of stoners where Staci was. They thought Laura was a narc so didn't want to talk to her, but after class one of them came up and told Laura that she was worried about

Staci too. "She told me Staci was getting in over her head with a new boyfriend," David read to Carolyn, "and that she was into harder drugs, and she was worried about her. She said the guy's name was Brandon and told me they were living together at the Oasis." Another rundown apartment block.

Carolyn said, "I remember Laura asked me go there with her one day. To find Staci. We went to the Oasis and waited around out front. Staci came out and we pretended to have bumped into her. Staci was thin. Already looked strung out. Laura was good at being non-judgemental—just said she missed her at school and wanted to hang out."

"Yeah, that's all here. It says she asked you because she knew you would say yes and she was scared to go alone. It says here you're a good friend, one of her best. There's more." David handed her the book, then looked away until Carolyn handed it back.

An entry from November said Staci was back in school. Laura brought extra lunch to give to her and invited her to hang out with them as much as she could, but Laura knew her friends and Staci didn't mix. She was also pretty sure Staci was drinking at school; she thought no one could smell the vodka.

Carolyn said, "I remember the weirdest thing. Staci always had one of those giant 7-Eleven cups. She was so small and thin that it looked like she had stolen a cup from the Friendly Giant or something. That was probably booze. Oh man, I was clueless back then."

In December, the entries became more about Laura and Jonathan breaking up. David skimmed through those into the new year. In January, a brief mention of continuing to be worried about Staci, who hadn't been to school after the break, and then some things on Trevor wanting to date her. She didn't think he was very smart but he seemed nice enough, so she went out with him.

David said, "Good Lord."

"What?"

"Ugh, I just… Trevor was good in bed, as it turns out."

Carolyn said, "I always wondered what she saw in him."

"He was the worst." David shut the book. "I don't need to know any of this. Could you look?"

He handed the book to Carolyn. She scanned the page, flipped, scanned. "Lots about Trevor…"

"I had no idea my sister even had sex."

"Girls had sex lives, just like you boys did."

"You're giving this boy too much credit. It wasn't until a couple of years after graduation that I 'knew' a woman."

Carolyn said, "Here's something."

In February, Laura wrote, Staci unexpectedly returned to school. She seemed to make an effort to catch up. Told Laura she didn't want to flunk out; she needed a diploma. Laura had gone to one of the vice principals and spoken on Staci's behalf without Staci's knowledge. He liked Laura, and she explained to him that Staci was a smart kid who'd just gotten into trouble. She talked him into letting her write an essay to make up missed marks. Laura helped her and was happy she seemed to be back on track.

The last entry, from early March, mentioned that Staci hadn't been to school that week and that Laura was worried about her again. She told her mom that she had a yearbook committee meeting and waited outside of Brandon's house. When she saw him leave, she knocked on the door and asked Staci if she was okay. If she needed anything. "She told me she was fine and didn't need me and I should go and not come back," Laura wrote. "She looked so thin. She was wearing a tank top and her shoulders looked like cue balls. She had scabs on her face and I think a black eye covered with makeup. I wanted her to come with me so bad, and then Brandon came back with another guy. They asked if I wanted to come in and party and Staci said I was just some girl trying to sell bibles. So I left, and I don't know if that was the right thing to do. I can't make Staci want to be better. I don't know what else there is to do."

"That's it," Carolyn said. "March 12." She shut the book.

"That's it," David repeated.

"What do you think?"

"It's probably nothing."

"But you feel like there's something."

"I don't know. There's nothing."

"But it *seems* like something. Maybe you could tell that reporter. They know how to ... shake things loose, I guess?"

David shook his head. "He'll make it a 'brother fingers old friend' thing. Like, I don't even know if this is anything. I'm not, like, Dixon Hill trying to solve a case."

"Dixon Hill?"

"He wrote pulp novels."

"I never read any."

"Me neither, but Picard would dress up as him on the Holodeck."

"That sounds like it's got to be *Star Trek*?"

"I recently rewatched some of the series, sorry."

"So."

"So."

"Well, I need to eat."

David said, "I have two slices of cold pizza and the last of my mom's earthquake stores."

"My parents have a flat of Kraft Dinner under the

counter for just such emergencies. Is that all you've been eating?"

David said, "...no?"

"Jesus. Let's go into town. I'll buy you dinner and we can talk more."

CHAPTER TWENTY

IN 1910, CONRAD MCALLISTER built a warehouse across from the town's train station. He used it to store and repair farm equipment and carriages. When cars came to the valley, McAllister saw the change coming and turned his warehouse into a garage and showroom. An oversized photo of the original Griffiths Garage hung in the hallway of the current Griffiths Garage, which had been renovated ten years before. The main floor had a used bookstore, organic market, and coffee shop. David waited in line, staring at the photo.

The building had been used as storage for decades and was completely abandoned by the time a local entrepreneur bought it at a tax default auction in the eighties. He found it filled with things now considered antiques.

He hung a sign outside that said "Rob's Quality Goods" and did very well the first few years—he sold a Model T and a few other genuine antiques he'd found buried in the garbage of the place. But by the time David started going there in high school, it had become a junk store. In grade twelve he would skip school to dig through the vinyl. In the early aughts, the junk store guy sold to developers, who branded it The Garage. Another photo showed the remodelling and grand reopening.

David ordered a coffee and went outside. Chairs lined the sidewalk, facing the cenotaph park and train station. The upstairs of the garage had been turned into office space and a dance and yoga studio. Staci Greene taught a yoga class there from 10:30 to 11:30. David had ten minutes to kill before it ended.

David and Carolyn had spent dinner talking circles around the subject of the video, Staci, and the book. They agreed it was probably nothing, but it was the sort of nothing that they had to know was nothing. The simplest way to know that it was nothing was to ask Staci what it was. They'd thought about messaging her, but if it wasn't nothing, it would be easy for her to say it was nothing over email. So, to make sure it was nothing, they'd have to talk to her in person. Carolyn offered to help, but David said, "No, it's nothing. I can track her down and ask what it was."

David had gone home and finally gotten his

cellphone out of the basement. After clearing out his junk emails and deleting everything from work, he had no messages. He went back upstairs and googled. "Staci Greene" didn't turn up anything. Carolyn had mentioned a yoga studio—he tried "Staci Griffiths Yoga" and got hits. The first, Valley Yoga and Wellness, was run by Staci Blake and had an Instagram account. The pictures were a mix of inspirational quotes—"Keep Calm and Do Yoga"—and a woman doing yoga poses around town. There she was in front of a totem pole stretching her arms. On top of the mountain with her heel tucked into her crotch. Prayer hands down at Fuller's Bay. The captions said things like "Always home, always beautiful" and "Manifest your own peace." David found a photo that showed her face close enough to confirm it was Staci.

Twenty years earlier, she'd always worn jeans and a plaid shirt, all baggy. She had been thin, but the clothes hid it. She was still thin, but the yoga clothes emphasized curves and muscles. Her hair, mousey blond in David's memory, was now an even, shiny blond. Her eyelashes, like her poses and her clothes, were perfect. Her Instagram went back eight years, all in Griffiths. It had occurred to David that he must have seen her around town for years and not recognized her.

Her Instagram linked to a website for Heartland Farm, where you could do yoga and wellness retreats and workshops. The workshop descriptions talked about "Manifesting Your Higher Self" and "Awakening." The retreats all centred around meditation, yoga, and doing farm work as a way of reconnecting with nature. The prices seemed scandalous. The "About Staci" section said that she was a born-and-raised "Valley Girl." After leaving home as a teen to live in Vancouver, she'd returned with her beloved husband and a new focus on wellness and the body. She had manifested, she wrote, a home that represented her inner being and the peace she hoped to attain and share with others. She was a licensed yoga practitioner and worked at the local studio.

David had texted Carolyn a link to the website and written, "For a mere $500 you can spend a weekend doing Staci's gardening."

She'd written back, "Hey, you got your cellphone finally. Call me after you talk to her. Good luck."

A woman in yoga clothes and a mat rolled up under her arm came out of the coffee shop. David put his phone away and watched the door. More came out, alone or in pairs, chatting. Some stopped for coffee. They loaded into cars all around. Large new suvs. Mostly black. Only one of the women got into the sort of hippie van David expected yoga women to drive. He watched another woman let her dog out of a car and let it run around the park. And then Staci came out with a big backpack and an old-style boom box under her arm.

He caught up with her at the train tracks and said, "Staci?"

She turned around. She looked suspicious, pulled the boom box between herself and David. She said, "Yes?"

David said, "David, David McPherson."

She said, "Oh" and then closed her eyes. She opened them slowly, a smile coming as she did. Her whole body seemed to lift. She said, "What a welcome surprise to be brought together today."

David said, "Yeah, it's been a while."

She put a hand on his elbow. "How are you." The emphasis on "are" was heavy. Her head tilted and she stared into his eyes, unblinking. "I saw about your mother. I'm so sorry. You're in town because of her?"

"Actually, I've never not been in town. I thought you'd left?"

"I did, for a while, but I was drawn back here nearly ten years ago."

"This is going to be weird, but I actually googled you." Her smile slipped. David had come up with several ways to approach this, none of them good and all of them now forgotten. He said, "So, actually, some of Laura's old friends got in touch when my mom died and we got to talking about my sister. Your name came up a couple of times, so I started to wonder where you ended up." Staci tilted away. David remembered one of the lines he'd thought would work on her, based on all the New Age stuff on her Instagram. He said, "I've been seeking closure on some things since my mom died and would appreciate it if we could talk. I know you and my sister were close."

She said, "That must be why we were brought together. Let's sit."

David followed her across the tracks to the Dutch bakery that he had never set foot in but which was the town's oldest business. Staci ordered a tea, David a coffee. She said, "Let's go out back," then slipped behind the counter and down a hallway. David followed her but felt like they shouldn't be back there.

A steel door opened into a courtyard. There were brick walls on four sides, covered with climbing ivy, a small fountain, and wrought-iron chairs and tables. None of the buildings in downtown Griffiths were taller than three storeys; most were only two. David had always assumed they went back all the way to their neighbours, so that each block was solid building. It had never occurred to him that there could be courtyards. Staci sat down at the table in the far back, against the wall. They were the only ones there.

"I had no idea this was here."

"I would come here back in high school. It was a place to centre myself then. And I come here now when

I need a minute to reconnect or calm. I'm usually the only one here." She closed her eyes and breathed in. The smile came back; she looked like she was going to present a cupcake to a toddler.

"You seem a lot different than I remember," David started.

"It's funny," she said. "When I first moved back to the valley, I avoided town — Trent and I live out in Shawnigan, we do our shopping in Victoria. It wasn't like I moved back *here*." She gestured around them. "But then I decided to confront the past — blaming a place for actions of the self was shifting responsibility. To return here and face the negativity has been an important part of finding my higher self. And the thing is," she said, "it wasn't as bad as I'd thought." She smiled her secret smile again. "You are your own worst memory of yourself," she said. "One of the people in my yoga class was in my grade in high school. She doesn't remember me at all. No one seems to. I skipped class so much back then, most people here never knew me. And it wasn't me back then anyways. I have awakened since then; it's all behind me now."

"About that," David said, "I know my sister tried to help you out...when you were, you know, not doing so great."

"I don't like to talk about that time. It's all still a part of me, and a necessary part of my growth, but it's not who I am. Things happen," she said, "so you can become the person you are meant to be."

"Right. It's just, I don't really remember you leaving town. I guess I had other things on my mind. But did you go right after Laura died?"

"That summer, yes. I moved to Vancouver."

"And you were seeing that guy Brandon, right? You move together?"

Staci's face tightened. She said, "We did but we broke up soon after. I'd prefer not to talk about it. My time in Vancouver was a trial I had to endure, but it led to me meeting Trent and finding myself; from bad comes good."

The second time she said her husband's name it clicked for David. He said, "You married the Tim Hortons guy?"

"He's getting out of the doughnut franchise to focus on his development projects." David remembered the stories about him sleeping with the doughnut girls. "He's a partner in the company that is building the new golf course out on the south end of Shawnigan. And they've been doing the different phases of the Mountainside, out by where you used to live."

David felt a grasping that comes when a meaningless coincidence seems like something more. To fill the space and let himself think, he said, "How'd you meet him?"

"He came to the bar I worked at when he was on the farm team in Abbotsford. We were both lost at the time. His hockey career was ending and he couldn't see a future without it. But together, we planned out a future. He introduced me to healthy living, working out, yoga. And I introduced him to a spiritual side, how to envision and manifest a future, how to become the life you want.

"It's funny, actually, because I probably wouldn't have dated him if I'd known he was from Griffiths. He'd left here to play junior hockey in Ontario, and whenever he talked about growing up, it seemed like he was from out east. But after we were together eight months he said I should meet his parents. They live out in Arbutus Bay and we hung out near the ocean and hiked up the mountains and I saw for the first time how pretty it is here. He had a nice family. It was just such a different experience than I remembered. So, it was actually my idea to move back. We needed somewhere to start our life together. Moving here was the choice, to make a fresh start." Her eyes closed again and her body centred. "But you wanted to talk about your sister, not me," she said.

"Right," David said. He sipped his coffee to buy time. Put it down. Spun the handle to one side. Then the other. He said, "I was just... A lot of people have been talking to me about my sister and I've heard things that surprised me. I guess, you know, I was her little brother and I saw her a certain way. Like, she had this whole life separate from harassing me and telling me my shows were stupid or I needed to shower or whatever. I guess that's probably obvious, but, you know, I don't think about it that often."

"You learn what you're supposed to, when you are meant to learn it. You can't beat yourself up for ignorance, only the unwillingness to learn."

"That's what I always say. But I suppose what I'm wondering about is how she offered to help you."

"As I said, I don't like to talk about that time." Her face was hard again, but then softened as she considered. "But you are looking for something, I can tell. So, let me tell you this. Your sister had a good heart and wanted the best for everyone."

"But she showed up to try to get you away from those guys? Right?"

"I can't remember."

"She stopped by Brandon's house and tried to get you to come with her."

Staci said, "Your sister always said she wanted to help me, but she had no idea what I was going through then. She had no idea the things I had to put up with as a poor kid who everyone knew had no protection. Do you even know what that was like?"

David was caught off guard. Her tone had changed;

the considered hippie welcomeness was gone. She sounded more like he remembered.

"I'm going to tell you a story. Your sister always tried to get me into sports. I went along with it in middle school because rugby was fun and I could knock around rich girls. But then in high school there was no rugby, so she talked me into playing basketball. And one month in, Mr. Gregg, that pervert basketball coach, came up behind me and tried to get a hand in me. And do you know what I could do about it? Nothing. I knew by then that no one was going to help me. The school would protect its guy. He'd been doing that since 1968 and everyone knew. So I had to quit.

"People know who they can get away with that with. I learned that pretty quick. And your sister never had to learn that, so she didn't know. You guys had your comfortable little lives like most people around here and couldn't see beyond it. So look. Your sister showed up and said she would help me. But what could she do? Your mom hated me. I couldn't go to your place. She offered to give me like, a hundred and fifty dollars from selling lemonade or whatever, and that wasn't going to get me very far. So I told her no. And to stop coming by. She didn't understand my world, then—she didn't know what I had to do. And it wasn't a big fucking deal. She wanted to 'save' me or whatever, but what I needed was an entirely different life."

229

Staci stopped. Placed both palms down on the table and breathed in. She said, "I keep saying I don't like to talk about that time, but it's not because I'm ashamed or did bad things or whatever. It's because that's not me anymore. I left here. I went to Vancouver. I got rid of Brandon. My real life found me."

"What ever happened to Brandon?"

"He died."

"I'm sorry."

"Whatever. He overdosed or killed himself or something a couple of years after we broke up. I hadn't spoken to him in years and I only found out a year after it happened. Look, I hope you can find what you're looking for, but I don't think I can help you. I should leave."

David said, "Why did you take one of Laura's diaries at her funeral?"

"What?" She stopped, half-crouched out of the seat.

"You took a book out of our house after the funeral."

"I don't know what you're talking about." She sat back down.

"I was going through some old news footage of the funeral reception. It shows you going into the house and coming out with a book, and you get into that Ranger guy's Camaro."

"I don't remember a book. Or a diary. Maybe I was taking back something I lent her?"

David said, "I'm just trying to figure out why you'd sneak in to get a lent book. Why not ask?"

"I can't remember, but I'd guess I didn't want to ask your parents. They thought I was trash."

"And why get a ride with Ranger?"

"Brandon was away, Ranger was a friend."

"Where was Brandon?"

"What does that matter? It was twenty years ago." Staci closed her eyes. She straightened her spine. Seemed to count up the vertebrae, stacking each on top of the other, her eyes opening like the tip of a whip after they were aligned. Her voice came down a register, the harshness left her. She said, "It broke my heart when your sister died. She was a good person who wanted to help. But she died for a reason. I don't know what you're looking for right now, but I don't think I have what you think you need. But I can tell you some things.

"It may be hard for you to face this, but your sister died so that you could become who you are today. Holding onto the past will keep you there; you need to be free. Laura gave us a gift. It took me some years to see that. But once I opened myself to that gift, I was able to awaken and find my higher self.

"I feel like you are close to attaining this. You are here, asking me questions I don't have the answers to. You are inquiring, which is the first step to awakening. Your mind and soul are close. I know" —her secret smile was back—"what this moment is like. I know how easy it is to block things out. But our synchronicities have brought us together. It is a sign you can't ignore. You must focus on today—if you want to honour your sister and her sacrifice."

CHAPTER TWENTY-ONE

ROBERT GRIFFITHS, WHO BUILT the train station that the town was built around, sold his land off in pieces. His orchard became the downtown, his barley field the Chinatown. As the town grew, he, and then his sons and grandsons, sold off his fields one by one. The Griffiths family had been allotted the ground on the river floodplain, between the river and a small lake, when they settled. As the town expanded into that land, a dike was put in to control the flooding. As the town grew, more and higher dikes went in, and the river became no more than a straight ditch through town. This had caused the river water to move so fast that the creeks from the lake couldn't drain into it, which in turn caused the water level in the lake to rise, flooding the remaining farmland around it and creating a huge swamp just outside of town. In the last couple of years, the city had rebranded the bog as "The Wetlands" and turned it into a park with raised trails and a viewing platform. The new ecosystem had attracted many species of birds.

Carolyn had seen the new park on her way into town and suggested meeting there after David talked to Staci. She texted, "Better to talk in person and I want to see how they spruced up the old bog." David wrote back, "I'll grab coffees."

David sat at a picnic table near the park entrance. It was thirty feet from the highway and he could hear the cars thrumming by. Trails led out of the clearing into underbrush that was mostly dead and grey. There was no view of the lake. Carolyn looked around as she walked toward him. She sat down said, "This isn't much of a park."

"Apparently a lot of people live in it, too. My mom wouldn't come here because she didn't want to get 'clopped on the head' for her purse."

"Your mom never struck me as a hiker."

"Not once in all the years I knew her did I know her to go for a hike. She did like to read the local paper though, and people sure do like writing letters to the editor complaining about the homeless people ruining the beautiful park they hadn't wanted the city to spend money on one year earlier. People here are fun."

"I have never again," Carolyn said, "lived in a town where everyone worried so much about everyone else's business. My dad was obsessed with that kind of thing when I was a kid. There was something about a creek and the gravel pit?"

"My dad went to the town archives for the only time in his life to research his complaint about that one. But this has been a real nightmare. When they built the park they wanted to put in a trail right around the lake, but there was some confusion with old property deeds. The muni had an old agreement that any land within thirty feet of bodies of water was theirs, but the owners on the far side of the lake had old deeds that said things like 'the property extends four hundred feet from the edge of Lansdowne Road.' And since the lake shore is now an extended bog, there were a lot of arguments about it. My mom kept me up to date every week on what 'everyone was saying on Facebook.' Anyways, they didn't build the trail in the end, but they did build a viewing platform. It cost a million dollars and I'm sure you can imagine the letters in the paper about spending that kind of money on a platform."

"Oh, God."

"Weird town," David said, "where someone's tree hanging onto your yard can make the front page of the paper, but a teenage prostitution ring is just a fun local secret."

A man pushed a shopping cart into the picnic area. He looked in a garbage can and then the recycling. He took out three cans and put them in a plastic bag.

"Let's walk," Carolyn suggested. "I want to see this million-dollar view, and you can tell me how things went with Staci."

They checked the map that welcomed them to the wetlands and let them know YOU ARE HERE. A series of trails crossed each other and went to different habitat displays. All of them led to the viewing platform eventually. David and Carolyn walked into brush up over their heads. Small green buds were coming in over the dead brown and grey bramble. The path felt like walking down a hallway.

Carolyn said, "This feels like a maze."

"I hear the Minotaur is very friendly."

They walked a minute and Carolyn prompted, "So."

"So." David sighed. "It was weird."

"Oh?

"Staci seems to think my sister died so she could marry an adulterous hockey jerk and join, or possibly lead, some kind of yoga cult."

"Holy shit."

"I mean, I was expecting it to be a weird conversation, but not that kind of weird."

"Yeah, shit. Did you find out anything?"

"She said Ranger gave her a ride to the funeral

because Brandon was away. She doesn't remember any book, but I'm not sure I believe her. When I tried to ask her directly, she was sketchy and shut it down. She did, however, suggest I open myself to universal synchronicities to be a whole human or something like that."

"Well that's not very helpful."

"Really? I think the astral plane is a nice place to be. I don't think Staci was high, but she seemed high, you know? Can't be too bad."

"I mean the stuff about the book."

"Not a lot of help there, no."

They stopped at a fork in the trail. Neither could remember which way they were meant to go. David tried to look over the top of the brambles for a clue and decided on left. In the bush, they could see a bright tarp and tent that would be hidden when the leaves grew. There was an open, empty set of luggage worn by the elements a little farther on.

David said, "She did say some stuff about what she had to deal with, growing up here and poor."

"Yeah?"

"She said Laura didn't get it because we were rich, but it would never have occurred to me that we were rich. Like, the way my dad talked about things affecting his property value, how much it cost to drive into town, how much just...whatever...I thought we were always just on the verge of losing the house."

"I get it all the time when I talk to people about my work. People who are comfortable fundamentally don't get the differences in ... anything, really. Like, maybe when they were teenagers they worked a minimum-wage job for a summer and it was tough to make rent, and that becomes their whole worldview. 'I got out of being broke, so can anyone.' But of course, these people were always at least a bit comfortable. At least, further from living in shelters than people I deal with."

"I never really thought about it."

"Because you don't have to."

"I guess." David snapped off a bramble off and broke it into smaller and smaller pieces. He said, "Staci remembered Laura coming to 'save' her or whatever, but thought it was pretty much a joke that a hundred dollars and some goodwill could help her in any way."

"Prayers and sandwiches," Carolyn said. "I mean, we really were sheltered from some of the things that were happening all around us."

They had, by then, taken several turns and walked suddenly into a small clearing with a large, square viewing platform in the middle. They climbed the stairs. At the first landing they were above the treeline, and at the top there was a view of the boggy land and then open water. The algae was mostly gone or stuck to the edges, so the lake was clearer than David had ever seen it. Across it were the old farms — a section of town not yet built up—and behind it all, the mountain.

"This is pretty nice, actually," David said.

Carolyn said, "Not that nice." She faced the other way, toward town. The highway was right there, buzzing. A cloud of smog hung over it all. She joined David on his side of the platform.

"What are you thinking?" she said.

"I don't know. I guess it was all nothing. Even if Staci knew anything, what would it matter? It doesn't change anything. Something cruddy happened. I don't know." David broke a stick he'd been fidgeting with in half and threw a piece off the platform. He watched it fall. He said, again, "I don't know."

Carolyn looked at him a minute, and then out over the bog. "Can I tell you what I think?"

"Please."

"I used to think, a lot, about who could have done that to your sister. Like, for years after, I would drift off and think of everyone in town and your sister and how they connected. For a long time, I thought it had to be someone at school. Someone she knew. There were maybe a dozen guys in our graduating class who could have done it. A dozen. Maybe John Sherman, on the corner. He killed cats when we were kids. He would stare at girls he liked. He was a creep. Or maybe Trevor—like, maybe they tried to break up and things got out of hand. Or maybe the redneck kids who four-by-foured up on the mountain could have been driving by and saw a chance. There were so many possibilities. So many guys who, if you told me they did it, I'd have said, 'Makes sense.'

"And that's a scary sort of thing, you know? And then I got older and saw more of the world, and the kinds of things that were going on in Vancouver when I was there. That was the height of the pig farmer years, right before they caught him. Once I started working on the Downtown Eastside and getting to know people, they would tell me about friends of theirs who were just gone one day. Everyone down there knew something was up and they tried to tell people but no one listened for years and years. A girl even got away once and told the cops and they went down and checked out the farm but let the guy off. He said they were just partying and it got out of hand. There's so much space for a guy to get bad. So much is ignored.

"It's like this Sanderson guy, who assaulted my client. We found out he was married twenty years ago and his wife died. He brought her to the hospital. She was unconscious, smashed in the head from, he said, a horse. She died without waking up. The police questioned him about it but let him go. There had been rumours at the time, but nothing was done. And maybe a horse did kick her head in. Or maybe he lost his cool with her and it got out of hand and because he's a guy who looks a certain way and has certain resources, he got away with it. Hard to say, but we found out his second wife reported him for assault three times and had to get a restraining order after she left him. He was allowed to get away with it, and that's not even to mention what was never reported. What we don't know about.

"And so he knows he can get away with things, and he gets a chance to do something awful with someone he thinks no one will miss. And if she hadn't gotten out, would we ever know? I'd have a client who was missing. I'd file a report. The police would look at it and think 'sex worker, no fixed address, addict, not worth our time,' and then no one would ever think of her again. Even if her body did turn up, no one would care because she worked a 'high-risk' job.

"Sorry," she said, "I'm going on. What I mean is that in our society there's a permissible level of violence, sexual or otherwise, that is systemically ignored. And the line is unclear to many until they've crossed it, because no one ever corrects it. At school you can push a kid into a locker and a teacher will laugh it away. But if you duct-tape a kid to an upright and leave him, then you get in trouble."

David said, "Actually, they didn't get in trouble."

"Really?"

"It was the last day of school. The principal said he couldn't do anything about it. In fact, he said he and his buddies had done the same thing to a kid when they were in school and he never stopped to consider how the kid felt about it. This was to me, hyperventilating in his office. I think he wanted me to say it was okay he'd been a dick in high school. Anyways, nothing was ever done."

"So, exactly. Where the line is drawn is never clear. It wasn't drawn for those guys, and then they went on to do their things. Some were corrected along the way, others weren't. One ended up in jail because he thought what he did was fine; another figures it out and becomes the top BMW salesman in Australia."

"Austria," David corrected.

"But all those guys got second and third and fourth chances," she said. "One of them ran out of chances and ended up in jail, another guy became a success, but does he still have the potential to do something awful? Does that go away? The way it seems to happen in my line of work is that some things are normalized, and when they are, people find the potential to do a thing they might not have before.

"So," Carolyn said, "that's what I think happened to Laura. She just ran into someone at the wrong time. It could have been literally anyone. People drove around the mountain; someone could have just happened to be at the gate. Just coincidence. And maybe it was someone she knew or maybe not. And maybe they said something dirty to her and she said she'd tell and then it got out of hand. Or maybe she saw someone coming out of the woods on drugs or something and they tried to scare her. It could have been a hundred different things, but it would have started small, because a guy thinks he can behave a certain way, and maybe Laura pushed back and then he goes farther and realizes he could be caught and named. It escalates to the point where he's gone too far because he crossed a line he never thought about."

David had broken the rest of the stick into small pieces, which were lined up along the railing. He swiped them off. He said, "Once when I was hiking up the mountain, I came across a grow op. I didn't know what it was then. I was like, twelve? Anyways, there were these weird plants and I walked through this clearing and suddenly a guy was there, at the edge of the clearing. He told me to keep walking and he seemed a bit scary, but I would run into people sometimes on the trails so I didn't think much of it until, like, four years later, when I realized it must have been a guy watering or checking on the crop. I guess if I'd been older or, like, a girl, that could have gone differently. He might have tried to intimidate, like you said, and who knows."

"Exactly," Carolyn said. "I never climbed up that mountain alone because who knows who I'd run into.

But you and your friends could go up and down, get lost on it, no problem."

Carolyn looked over the swamp. David turned around to look back at the highway. Two police cars pulled into the park, followed by an ambulance. The ambulance drivers pulled a gurney out of the back, chatted with the cops, and disappeared from view. Carolyn had joined him. She said, "I wonder what that's all about?"

"They don't seem to be hurrying, but maybe we should head back."

They climbed down the stairs and walked into the bramble trail. Carolyn said, "So."

"So. I guess it's nothing.

"But you still think it's something."

"I don't know. It's something, but it's probably not something that matters. Like, maybe Staci thought Laura wrote something possibly incriminating about her—maybe that she was doing sex work. And maybe Staci didn't want that to get out and get her boyfriend in trouble."

"That's definitely possible."

"What else could it be? I mean, for a minute it seemed like there was something. But I guess it's just... nothing."

They took a different trail back and made it to the picnic area and parking lot within a minute. A cop was standing by their cars. He saw them and walked over.

"These yours?" They nodded. "Anyone else with you?" They shook their heads. The cop pressed the little microphone clipped to his lapel and spoke into it. "The people in the cars are accounted for. You should be all clear in there."

David said, "What's going on?"

"An investigation," he said, officially. And then less officially, "A couple birdwatchers found a body in there." David realized it was the cop from the roadblock a few days before.

"Jesus."

"Nothing to worry about. Just one of the homeless. That Jake Holmstead guy who's been missing."

"Weren't you guys looking in the river for him? There was a helicopter?"

"Yeah, someone said they saw a body in the river, and he was missing so we thought it might be him. But I guess he was out here the whole time. Body is pretty well rotted. A lot of the homeless live out here. We clean them out every now and then, but they come back. You build a nice park and it gets so people can't even come into it. They're scared. And why not. These guys'll stick you up. My mom lives in the home downtown. She can't even sit out in the park without one of them hitting her up for change. It's a travesty."

David said, "So there's still a body in the river?"

245

"Who the fuck knows? These junkies are dropping like flies. I got better things to do than fish them out of wherever they fall."

"Right. Have yourself a good day."

"You too."

The cop got into his car and took out his phone. David and Carolyn walked to their cars. She said, "Cops don't even try to not be complete shits."

"They're all that bad?"

"In my experience they are either useless or they actively make things worse. The only time they say anything is when something gets solved and they can pretend to be heroes. Anyways. This was a lot, today. Are you okay?"

"Yeah, I guess."

"What now?"

"I don't know. I guess nothing. I have to sort out all my mom's stuff. Someone's coming by tomorrow to look at the place. I might sell it, I guess. I don't need all that space."

"Where would you move?"

"I have no idea. Honestly, I don't know what I'm doing at all."

"If you need help with anything you can call me. If you want to talk things out. Maybe we can talk about... I don't know, houses or something? What do regular adults talk about?"

"The market. The economy."

"Oh, the economy. Love that economy." She gave him a hug and said, "Give me a call when the apocalypse food runs out. We'll have lunch."

CHAPTER TWENTY-TWO

DAVID GOT HOME AFTER dark. He'd driven aimlessly. Up into the mountains on the logging roads and ending up in a village in the middle of the island. He took the newly paved road from there to the west coast and drove south along the road that skirted the Pacific. He got out for the sunset and wondered why he didn't go out that way more often. He came back through the suburbs of Victoria, thought about driving in for a meal but then figured he should get home. The night was clear, and coming into his valley the houses up his mountain looked like stars.

A note tucked into his door turned out to be from James. It said that he knew David was reluctant to talk and he understood. He was sorry to be a bother, but he did have one thing he wanted to give David. He explained that David's mom had wanted David to have the recordings of the interviews she gave. He would put them on a USB key and drop them off the next afternoon, at one. He hoped he could talk to David then.

David went inside and turned on his mom's computer. He typed "Brandon Richardson" into the search bar on his mom's browser, and when the Bing results came up he went to Google and searched again. He added "Griffiths," and the name of his high school. There was a graduation record—ten years before David; nine years older than Staci, then. The next hit was an obituary.

The picture of Brandon would have been from high school, but he died in 2005. The obit said only that he was taken too young and had had a difficult life. He'd been survived by a mother and grandparents. David searched the mother's name. She was still alive and lived in the valley. He found her address; it was on the same road as the Sanderson farm. For a second, David thought it meant something. But it had to be just another coincidence; the town wasn't big.

He tried searching for "Ranger" and "Griffiths," then "Ranger Griffiths Pool Hall," and then "Ranger Griffiths Arrest." The last one turned up something. The links went to a site where he could read scanned and archived back issues of the local paper. There was no way to search, so he read the whole thing. A fire at the mill. Kindness strikes a chord at a local concert. First Nation claims church land should be returned. New doctor needed. Stay back from gravel trucks to avoid damage to your car. Local man raising money for poverty in Tibet. And then an article about a murder. In 2004, Matthew "Ranger" Donaldson had killed a guy near Shawnigan Lake. The police said Ranger had taken a guy out to the woods and run into him with a truck. Ranger's lawyer claimed they had been drinking and decided to goof around and truck surf, which is when you stand on the hood of a four-by-four when it's moving. The guy fell off and got crushed between the truck and a tree. The jury seemed to think there was enough reasonable doubt that Ranger was let off with manslaughter and time served.

David searched "Matthew Donaldson," then "Matt Donaldson." He tried adding a few terms to narrow the search. He ended up on an interactive map of unsolved cold-case murders and suspicious disappearances in BC, published by the CBC. There were dots on a map you could click; a short summary of the case popped up.

Matt Donaldson's body had been found outside of Kelowna with obvious signs of trauma. He had lived in the city for a decade and had a criminal past. He was last seen the night before, driving his truck out of town. A photo of Ranger's mugshot from the manslaughter case topped the article. Leads were requested.

David moused over the island. There were dozens of dots around the valley, with dates starting in the 1960s. A hippie who wandered into the woods in the 1970s and was never seen again. A man with no known criminal connections, found dead in the woods two hundred metres from his truck, which had blood in it. Three Jane Does over thirty years found with stab wounds in the Wetlands, the end of the river canyon, and behind the old Superstore. On the reserve, six women missing, thought not to have run away; there were no details beyond names. He hovered over his house and his sister's graduation photo popped up. He shut down the browser.

The interviews David had downloaded from his mom's email were saved on the desktop. He clicked on the second one.

James asked if they could talk a bit about Laura herself. What she'd been like. Her friends and hobbies. The kind of stories David always heard. Honour roll. Volunteer. Kind. The anecdotes and memories that would fill up the article. His mom sounded happy to share the stories. They had been told before and came easily. David jumped ahead, listened, and jumped ahead again.

They were talking about the night she went missing. David's mom said, "I knew, right away, that something had gone wrong. You can sense it, you know. A feeling." His mom had always said that, about the night Laura went missing. It wasn't true. They'd watched two full episodes of *Home Improvement* without realizing she was gone.

His mom went over the night and the days after. The order of events, the stories he'd heard. David jumped ahead, listened a little, jumped ahead.

James was trying to pin down dates and his mom couldn't remember. She said, "You know, I've got a box of stuff you can have. It's all the old clippings and some letters and that kind of thing. It'll have the dates better than I can remember."

"That'd be great."

"There's some other stuff in there too, some silly stuff. For a while I was reading these theories about Laura's death. There are these websites. People talk about it."

"I've actually read some of those."

"They're nonsense. It's like a hobby for some people, spending time trying to figure out these old murders. But for a while I spent some time on them. You know, it was mostly wild theories, but some people seemed to actually care about her as a person, as opposed to just as someone who got killed. And it was nice to read that sort of thing."

"I can imagine it's hard that you never got to see what she would have become."

She thought a long time, then said, "You know, she was eighteen. It's impossible to know. I mean, eighteen is young. If you'd asked me, at eighteen, what I would become, I would have thought I'd be living in London or Paris and travelling the world as an artist. My mom would have thought that maybe I'd move to Vancouver. You don't know. Look at Laura's friend Becky—she wanted to act. She was in all the plays, and I think she was pretty good. But that didn't happen for her. Between one thing and another she didn't even get to university. And that could have been Laura just as easy. I'd like to think not, but you can never know how a kid will turn out. But that's just the thing. Good or bad, I would have liked to have known." The recording ended shortly after that.

David opened the third recording; the one from the night his mom died. A Tuesday. David had gotten off work, eaten some takeout, and, since he had the opening shift the next day, had just watched a movie and scrolled through the internet. He'd heard a murmur from upstairs, knew his mom was talking, assumed it was to a friend.

James said, "One of the things we haven't gotten to talk about yet is the effect Laura's death had on the people around you. It was such a big thing in town, and my family, even, was changed by it." He caught himself and added, "Obviously not as much as yours..."

"It's fine. I know what you mean. People tell me that. I got letters, for years, about it. They were always very kind, and they wanted to share how Laura had affected their lives. Harold didn't care for it, but I think I understood. She was our daughter, but her death became something that happened to the town."

"That's exactly it. It was the first time I really saw that there was bad in the world. My mom and dad got worried. My older sister wasn't allowed out suddenly. They picked her up from school and dropped her off. She started getting angry about it, fighting with my parents all the time, and I think it was a big part of why she ended up going to school in Toronto. She wanted to get away from my parents, who were just reacting to feeling unsafe. And I was a bit younger and didn't really understand it at all. I thought we lived in, like, a little paradise."

David's mom considered a moment, then said, "You said you grew up on Arbutus Bay?"

"That's right."

"Did you go to Griffiths High?"

"No, we went to Inglewood."

Inglewood was a private school south of town. Students from across the country boarded there and rich locals went as day students. There was a one-sided rivalry between Inglewood and the public high school; the jocks in David's school had been obsessed with beating Inglewood. Their basketball team was coached by an ex-Olympian, their soccer team by a real European. The kids had all the time and equipment needed to get good, and they always crushed the public school teams. David saw this happen once — the basketball coach, Mr. Gregg, also taught David's math class, and he said he'd give anyone in the class two extra percent on their report card if they went to the game to support "our boys." David enjoyed the game more than he should have — it was fun to see the jocks lose so badly that they resorted to fouling Inglewood to try to hold on to some dignity. But then they got kicked out of the game. The results were the same with rugby and field hockey and track. Inglewood also had water polo, sailing, and rowing teams. The public school did not compete in those sports.

"And you said your parents are in Victoria now?"

"Yeah, that's right. We moved to Griffiths when I was six. Dad was management at the mill. They moved after I left for university."

"So," David's mom said, "you weren't really here too long. It's maybe a different place for different people. I mean, I grew up here. My dad did too. My grandpa was from out east but moved here when he was sixteen for work. We're not one of the homesteader families, but we've been here a hundred years, which is pretty good. So for me, it's maybe not the same place as you grew up in."

"I'd like to hear your thoughts on that, if you don't mind."

"What I mean is," she said, "well, people come here now because it's pretty and there's mountains and rivers and the ocean close by. If you don't mind the commute, you can get a big house and spend your weekends sailing or hiking or whatever it is people like to do. But it wasn't really like that back then. I mean, there were always forests here and rivers and it was always pretty, but before, it was more ... you got loggers and hunters and fishermen and whatever. The town was different. I mean, your family, these new people, they choose to live here. But for me and my family, it wasn't really a choice. Sorry." She paused a minute and seemed to think. "This isn't really what you want to talk about."

"No, no. I think it's interesting. Please, go on."

"I never really get a chance to talk about this, but I think about it sometimes. So I might not get it right. But, well ..." David's mom paused often between sentences. Seemed to search for memories and the words to put to them. She went on, "Like I said, my granddad moved here from New Brunswick, with a cousin, when he was sixteen. He got a job in the woods. They fed him. They gave him his own bed. It was a bunk, but before that he'd slept on a mattress on the floor with all his siblings and there was never much to eat, so his new life seemed like luxury. He worked as a topper for fifteen years and then hurt himself pretty bad and they let him drive the work crummy until he retired. He'd only gone to school until he was eight, but he did well enough in life that he had a little house, kids, a car. He never learned anything, but thought he had the world figured out because he did good in it.

"But he was," she said, "a nightmare. He was awful to grandma, to his kids. And it was because he didn't have the words. My dad told me how his dad would stutter, try to say something, and just turn red and start smashing things. He'd just never learned about feelings, putting words to them, dealing with them. He'd never had a chance. Not that I'm trying to be sympathetic—I didn't know him, but my dad and uncles never had anything good to say about him, and when he died it seemed like it was a relief to everyone.

"So there's my grandad, who moved here after the First World War, which was boom years, and people came to make money and every one of them was like my grandpa in some way. No education. Hard-working. Hard-living. You know, the logging industry always goes in these cycles, and when it's boom everyone is happy and things are easy and then it's bust and all these guys have nowhere to go and nothing to do and they're just... They're just here.

"And this is what my dad grew up in, during the thirties. It was harder out on the prairies, I think, but there wasn't much work here until the Second World War. My dad was too young for that, but a lot of guys went and not as many came back. Some died, but I think more of them saw the world and saw there was choice and didn't come back. I don't know that for sure. It's just what people say.

"So my dad really came of age right after the war. He'd only known being poor and then, suddenly, another boom hit. He and his brothers worked and made all kinds of money for the first time and they raised absolute hell. Growing up, I heard all the time about them. Sorry, I'm going on, you don't want to hear about my dad."

"Honestly, it's all good. Even if it doesn't go in the article, it's good to have background. Please . . ."

"Well, what I was going to say is they were goons, my dad and Uncle Mike." She laughed. "They always told these funny stories, but they're really not funny at all. They'd drive into the reserve and beat up Indians. They'd pick fights with out-of-towners. They had a little gang they hung out with. They just . . . they thought the world was theirs. You see it now in other places. Like the boys who go to Fort Mac. Becky's ex—please don't print this—but he goes there, works hard, wants to have a good time, and ends up with another family. It's terrible, of course, but you see it happen over and over.

"But with my dad, let me tell you. There was one story my dad always told about how he got into a fight with one of the Bradeys. I heard my dad and his friends tell it a hundred times, and they would laugh and laugh, but it's really actually horrible. The long and the short of it is, he beat the kid up so bad he ended up in the hospital, and a cop came to the house and told him that he could go to jail for that. The cop said they understood he was just out having fun — the Bradey kid wasn't much better — but he'd gone too far. If he ever had to come by again, the cop said, he'd arrest my dad. And that was all it took for my dad to straighten out a little.

"He had been working in the woods but transferred to the mill. He got to be management there. But this was long before your dad would have been there. It was a smaller outfit then, locally owned still. I mean this nicely, but my dad would have hated yours. He got retired early because he never finished school, and when the conglomerate bought them out, they had this union requirement that certain jobs required certain qualifications. He was initially grandfathered in, but they did everything they could to get him out. He had worked there forty years then, so he was pretty well steamed to have these young guys with business degrees telling him how to do the job.

"But back to what I was saying. He straightened out, when he first got that job. He had steady work. He got married, had kids. Tried to be better than his dad in that regard. We never got hit much, but he still had a temper. But he thought, like his dad, that he had

260

the world figured out. That he'd beat it somehow, even though he just rode out a boom and was given a chance to straighten out. But he didn't see it that way and he was very judgemental of anyone who he thought hadn't figured it out, like him.

"This is what I grew up around. And all my friends. We were raised by these men who were just... They thought they were something, but they only knew here. They'd only been taught what you learn *here*. They were raised to be a way and no one corrected them. They were never shown options. They'd never been shown how to *be* anything else. And they didn't even know what they didn't know. They just thought they knew everything and could do anything and they taught their sons to be like that too. And it all starts out harmless enough but then...

"Put it this way. When I was in school around grade four or five, suddenly you had boys catcalling you, and then, when they were a bit older, they started grabbing you. It was like a performance. Say 'hi pretty lady,' grab a girl, everyone laughs, and everyone goes on their way. No one ever said anything or complained, and a lot of the older guys—the teachers and dads and even the moms—thought it was just the way things were, so it was allowed. But all us girls hated it.

"I'm not a feminist or anything—the idea that men and women are the same is nonsense. You see it more as you get older. Of course there's differences; you can't argue with that. But some of the things that started back when I was young led to worse things later on. And maybe that's a good reason to have been fighting the things that seemed innocent or like boys being boys.

"Because," she said, "as we got older we started going to parties, and boys and some girls started drinking or doing drugs or whatever. And that attitude no one thought much of—that catcalling, groping, laughing about it—carried on. But with the booze and with age, it was more aggressive, and maybe a girl was drunk, and no one paid much attention to the things that could happen if one of those guys got her in a car alone. We didn't call it 'date rape' back then, but that's what it was. We knew you had to be careful around certain boys, but even nice boys couldn't really be trusted. And some girls went along with it because they wanted to have sex but didn't want to be known to be wanting sex. None of us wanted to be forced, obviously, but it was hard to know who wanted what because no one ever talked about it, and there were no words for any of it.

"When people said 'rape' they were talking about a girl being pulled into the bushes by a stranger—the sort of thing that happened to Laura. And we all knew that was bad, but because we didn't have words for the other thing, we just..." She paused a long time and then repeated: "Nothing was done. It's just the sort of place this is.

"What I mean is, there is so much bad here and everyone ignores it. I did too. I mean, I knew it was bad but I tried to control it. To ignore it. I married Harold. He was a good man who didn't yell or hit, but he still was, you know, a man, so he had his ways. But we decided to raise a family and I wanted to do a good job and protect them. To do a little better than my parents, you know. So we got this place out here, out of town. I told you Harold hated it out here, but I liked it. I could control the types of kids the kids hung out with because it was out of the way. If there was someone I didn't like my kids hanging out with I could just say 'No, I can't drive you in,' 'No, I don't want them coming out here.' I thought it was a good way to protect them from the way the town could be. And because I protected my kids from it, I started to think maybe things were better than they had been. God knows, I thought that right up until I couldn't any longer."

There was a long silence. Then she said, "But it took me a long time to realize that, I suppose. After Laura died, I wanted to try to go back to the way things were. Our little better life out here. Harold wanted to move. I wanted David to live here, in the house he grew up in. So much had already changed; I didn't want any more. So we stayed here. And I don't know if that's a good thing. But that's what we did. I wanted to protect us. To keep hiding, I suppose. But everything is just how it always was."

There was another silence. She was sorry, she said, to have gone on like she had. He probably wouldn't be able to print much of what she'd said.

James said no, it was all good. It was important for him, for the story he wanted to tell, to have this kind of context. And that's when she asked if she could have the recordings. "I've told you," she said, "a lot of things I wish I could tell David. It's so hard to actually talk to him about this sort of thing. We're close, I would say, but it's hard to really talk to each other, you know?"

James said it wasn't a usual request. "The reason we don't do this is because then you get people saying they didn't like what they said..."

"I promise I won't even listen to them. I'd just like to have them. For David. He might like to hear them one day."

"I think I could do that."

The interview was an hour long. It would have been 9:30 p.m. when she finished, David figured. He had been downstairs, his movie ending. He heard his mom upstairs, through the uninsulated floor, moving around. He thought of going up after the movie ended, but it was ten by then and she was at her computer. She would have checked her email and then played a game of Candy Crush before she went to sleep. David didn't go up. Just after midnight, an hour after he meant to go to sleep, he turned off the TV and brushed his teeth and then heard something. He wasn't sure what it was, but it was unusual. An animal, he thought. He ignored it for a minute and then wondered whether maybe something had happened. He went into the laundry room, up the split level and then to the bottom of the stairs. A faint glow from her lamp could be seen. He said, "Mom?" And again, louder, "Mom." When she didn't respond after the second call, he went up.

CHAPTER TWENTY-THREE

THE RINGING LANDLINE WOKE David up. He picked up the base, looking for a way to lower the volume, then unplugged it. He turned on the TV and put on coffee.

"An arrest," the newscaster said, "in the confinement case in a town north of Victoria."

Dick Sanderson had been caught at the ferry terminal in Nanaimo. He had hidden under a blanket in the back of a friend's van. When David would go over to Vancouver for concerts in his teens, he'd do the same: lie on the floor of a van under some jackets to save twenty dollars. The ferries had cracked down on this trick, and someone spotted Sanderson. The police were called. They let the ferry load but held back the line Sanderson was in until last. Twenty minutes had passed between the car getting in line and the ferry loading, so the local news heard about the arrest over police radio and were there to film it. Police cars surrounded the van from seemingly every direction. Officers crouched behind open squad car doors with guns levelled. A police helicopter and tank were in the background. Sanderson got out of the van and lay down on the ground.

A police officer appeared on screen. He said, "Thanks to the brave work of our officers, we were able to bring the suspect in without incident."

The news switched over to a story about a homeless encampment in Victoria that had been served an injunction to move. The police were shown pulling down tents.

David saw a car pull into the driveway. It was a luxury suv with a large photo of the real estate agent Jonny Shawn airbrushed on the back half.

David splashed cold water on his face in the kitchen sink while Jonny Shawn came around to the front and rang the bell. On his way down the stairs, David took the plastic cover off the doorbell speaker and removed the battery. He opened the door. Jonny Shawn stuck his hand out; David put the battery in his pocket and shook it. Jonny Shawn said, "Do you want this gone, Dave?"

"I'm just sort of feeling things out."

"Well, it's a good thing you called Jonny Shawn."
David acknowledged the reference to his ad with a
nod. Jonny Shawn continued: "This is a hot section of
a hot market. I'm sure you know, things are exploding
around here. Foreign investors, commuters. They're
calling this the Brooklyn of Vancouver."

"I've heard that."

"Can we take a look around the lot, Dave?"

David slipped his shoes on and walked out. He said,
"It's three acres, technically, but we only ever used the
front yard and a bit of the back. Sorry about the mess."
David hadn't started the spring clean-up before his
mom died, and since then it had just gotten more out
of hand. David pointed out a shrub that grew over into
the neighbour's yard, and which his mom relayed complaints about each spring. "That's the edge of the lot."
They walked around the back of the house. A small,
dark backyard was there; it still had the aluminum
swing set and slide from when David was young. A few
feet behind that was a line of trees. "It doesn't get any
light back here, so we've never done too much with
it. I had a fort a few hundred feet into the woods, and
then the property ends at the cliff." Jonny Shawn nodded and David added, "Actually, the property marker
is on top of the cliff—my dad always said we owned
the first three feet of the mountain."

"That's great. I'll have to use that in the sell line."

They walked back to the front along the Sherman Road side of the property and went into the house through the side door. "Sorry about the mess," David said. "I'm packing."

David showed him the living room and kitchen. They went upstairs. Jonny Shawn was unfazed by Laura's room because, David realized, there was no reason for him to be fazed. David said "just a minute" before they went into his mom's room. He slipped in ahead. He dragged the blanket back up onto the bed and picked up the little plastic bits that had been torn off the medical equipment by the paramedics. There was nothing to be done about the small brown stain on the carpet; his mom had puked something up when he got into the room. He said, "Sorry, haven't been in here in a bit. Come on in." Jonny Shawn hardly looked.

"There's a suite in the basement," David said. They went through the laundry room into David's living room. Jonny Shawn glanced around without much interest. David said, "We had a guy living down here but he moved out and I haven't had a chance to clean it up."

"No no no. That's cool. I think I've seen enough. Anyone buying this will probably want to tear down the house anyways."

"Really?"

"No offence. We'll still have to stage it, maybe throw

a new coat of paint on to make it look decent — if a house looks rundown, they'll think the property is worth less. And I'll need somewhere to put the sandwich trays. People like to eat at open houses. The yard needs a clean too. All small costs, but they'll pay off."

"What do you think it's worth?"

"Well, like I said, it's a teardown. But all the property around here is subdivided, so . . ." He seemed to be tabulating in his head. "I'll have to double check the zoning, but say you can subdivide this into four lots. It's a beautiful neighbourhood, good for commuting to Nanaimo or Victoria. You got parks and whatever at the top. The Mountainside is desirable, and this is just outside. No view, but the land behind you is protected, so nature will always be there. And we can probably get a developer interested — a colleague sold a lot on Sherman to the people doing the Mountainside, so we'll start with them. I'd say you could get nine hundred K for this. I'd list for eight-fifty and you'll get bids. Might go for a million."

David said, "My parents paid, like, fifteen thousand for this."

"I hear that a lot these days." He paused. "So, what do you think, Dave? Do you want it gone?" He held out his hand.

. . .

DAVID DROPPED THE DOCUMENTS he'd been given on the coffee table. Jonny Shawn had already had them filled out with little Post-it Notes sticking out the sides where David needed to sign. David's only request was that Jonny Shawn arrange to throw out everything David didn't move out himself.

He texted Carolyn. "Actually do need to talk about real estate. Going to sell the place. What's Nanaimo like?"

"Holy! That's great. I have a friend who can help out I think. That's exciting."

"Cool, call you in a bit?"

"Happy to help." And then, a minute later another text: "Any thoughts on the Staci situation?"

"It's nothing."

"Going to talk to the reporter?"

"Don't know yet."

"Call if you need to."

A car pulled into the driveway. He looked at the time: still two hours before James had said he'd stop by. Becky got out of the car.

CHAPTER TWENTY-FOUR

DAVID OPENED THE DOOR before Becky got to it. She said, "I came to offer a sincere —"

"I'm selling the house. If you want to take anything of Laura's, you're welcome to it."

"You're selling?"

"My mom left Laura's room like it was. I don't know if you've been up there...? Grab whatever you want." He turned around and went up the steps. Becky followed him in. She stood uncertainly in the kitchen. He said, "Take some boxes up with you if you need them. I'll be in the basement." He left her standing there.

He went down to his suite and boxed up his stereo and speakers, but decided he wouldn't bother with the his ten-disc CD shuffler, which he hadn't used in over a decade, or the tape deck. Likewise, CDs and all but a few records could go — he had collected them when he was young because they were a cheap way to hear music back then, not because he was an audiophile. He mostly streamed now. His TV was old enough that he didn't care about leaving it. No other furniture or appliances down there were worth keeping. He ended up with a suitcase of clothes and decided to keep his old guitar and amp; he'd spent most of his first summer's pay on it the year after he graduated. He put what he wanted to keep on the split level, by the front door.

He went through the main floor quickly, put his mom's photo albums into a box — he'd go through them when he had more time to pull out the good photos. And with no sign of Becky, he went up into his mom's room, did a quick sweep. And then into the office, his old room. He found a box of tax receipts that went back to 1973. He found his dad's and sister's birth and death certificates, and his mom's birth certificate. He took those and a few other official documents, and then made a conspicuous amount of noise on his way down the stairs, hoping Becky would take the clue. He piled everything up by the door. He realized he now owned one carload of things.

He looked at the clock. James would be there in half an hour.

Becky came down with a box. Her eyes were blood-shot. She said, "Are you sure you don't want anything in there?"

"Positive."

She went up and down twice more. She put the boxes by the door and then said, "I thought you might want this. It was in the collage on the wall."

The photo was of David and Laura sitting at a folding table in their front yard. A sign in front of the table said "Lemonade, 25 cents." They had a pitcher of lemonade and a stack of cups. David was six, his sister eight. They had wanted money for something—David could not remember what—and their dad had refused and told them they had to learn to make money. A friend of Laura's had done a lemonade stand a few weeks before. They got some concentrate out of the freezer and a pitcher, a card table from the basement. Their mom and the German couple bought a cup, but that was it for hours; their street went nowhere, so got no traffic. They played in the front yard most of the day near the table and were about to pack it in when a logging truck came down the mountain. It stopped at the corner; the air brakes hissed. The driver honked his air horn twice at them and then hopped down. He opened up his Thermos and dumped the last of his coffee and told them to fill it up. He gave them a twenty. They had spent the whole night planning how to spend the windfall.

"Thanks," David said. He slipped the photo into a box.

"It looks like you're moving out right away?"

"Yup."

"So fast. It'll be sad to see the place go. It's a second home to me." She looked around the room. Took a breath. Prepared. "I think James was planning on coming by. He has some recordings—"

"I already have them. They were in my mom's email. And I'm going to give him the stupid box."

"Oh, that's so great. I'm glad you've come around. It's what your mom wanted."

David stared at her.

"You're going let him interview you too?"

David said, "Do you remember Staci Greene?"

"Of course. I see her around town all the time. She teaches yoga at the Garage."

"You're friends?"

"No, we haven't talked since high school. I don't even think she recognizes me. I barely recognized her. She was gone for years I think and then moved back. She married Trent Blake."

"Owns the Tim Hortons."

"That's right."

"My sister was pretty good friends with her back in the day, right?"

"She was, yes. Your sister was so good to people, you know. Always wanted to help."

"Staci needed help?"

"Oh yes." Becky's face grew serious. "She was in with bad people. Drugs, you know."

"Oh, I know them. So, you didn't hang out with her?"

"No, I only really knew her through your sister. I guess they'd been friends in middle school?"

"Yeah."

"Well, I couldn't really associate with anyone like that. I was on the Youth Action Committee back then, you know, with the police liaison officer?"

"Narc Club. I remember. Was Laura involved in that?"

"No, I think she had candy-striping the nights of our meetings. People called it Narc Club?"

"... Some people."

"Well, we weren't 'narcs.' We just wanted to make the school safer. I remember Staci had this terrible boyfriend who was selling drugs to kids in school. And he was in with those bikers, you know, who had girls go down to Fuller's Bay. She was one of them," Becky said. "You know, a hooker."

David said, "Sex worker."

"Pardon?"

"'Hooker' is kind of rude. Sex worker is preferred these days. And did everyone in town know about this but me?"

"What do you mean?"

"It just keeps coming up. Anyways, you guys narced on her?"

"It wasn't 'narcing.' We just wanted to keep bad things away from the school. But we never said anything about Staci because she was Laura's friend."

"Nice of you."

"But we did tell Constable Johnson about her boyfriend selling drugs. You know there was such a problem with it back then. Probably still is, but it's all legal now. I mean, it was good, because they arrested him because we never did hear of him again after. And Staci cleaned up."

"He died."

"Who?"

"Brandon, Staci's ex. Died in Vancouver. Drug overdose or suicide or something."

"Well, you see, you get into drugs that's what happens."

"Or you marry a millionaire hockey guy."

"Well, that's different. She was a victim back then. Why so many questions about Staci?"

"I just saw her in some old photos," David said. "And wondered what happened to her."

"Well," she said, "thanks for this. I'd just really like to say I hope we can keep in touch. I know we're not as close as—"

Becky was facing David and didn't see a police suv round the corner, then gun its engine up Mountain Road. Two more followed, then an ambulance They had their lights on, but no sirens.

David said, "You can call any time, Becky. I gotta run."

CHAPTER TWENTY-FIVE

THE DAY LAURA'S DISCMAN was found on the far side of the mountain, a police car drove by the front of the McPherson house, heading up Mountain Road. Two more followed.

David had been hiding down in the basement. It wasn't yet set up like it would be for the week of the search; he only had a folding chair in front of the TV. He spent the morning watching *Live with Regis and Kathie Lee*, and then *The Price Is Right*. He went upstairs for lunch and then grabbed the laundry he'd done that morning and went back down. The afternoon TV was never as good. He watched the news — mentioned at the end: the police still looking for tips in the case of a girl missing in a town an hour north of Victoria — and then a soap opera came on. It wasn't the one his mom and sister watched. He tried to get the other channel but couldn't get it clear with the bunny ears. He turned off the TV and poked around the basement. Jumped on a pogo ball a couple of times and put it back. He opened some boxes he'd already looked through. Then he opened the back basement door and looked out at the backyard. It was in shade and damp, like always.

The only way anyone could see him cross the yard would be from his parents' room or from the dining room, which was only used on holidays. He still felt exposed hurrying across and didn't relax until he was in the treeline. He followed the trail to his old fort. He didn't go out there anymore; the boards were covered with moss, and the newer two-by-fours he'd used years before to fix where the floor sloped had fallen to the ground, causing the whole fort to list again. He thought of climbing up but wasn't sure it would hold. Instead, he walked to the bottom of the cliff, which was really more of a rock ledge — it had seemed insurmountable when he was six, and the idea that it was a cliff stuck. He walked to where a jumble of boulders had fallen and climbed up, and then followed the trail that angled up slowly and would cross the face of the mountain. The fresh air felt good after four days inside.

David climbed until he came to the small stream he'd built a bridge across years before. The large branches he'd used were a jumble now, blocking the flow. A pond formed on one side and the creek overflowed around the entrance to the bridge. He found a narrow part of the stream to hop over.

The trail led to a fork where he could go either toward the top of the mountain or through a little valley and to the next mountain over. He stuck to his mountain, deciding to go as far as the first lookout and then head back down. It would take under an hour, which seemed a safe amount of time to be gone.

Ten minutes up, the trail suddenly gave way to a huge, empty space where the woods had once been.

Not empty. It was a clear-cut—which must have been done over the course of the early spring. A huge square of trees removed. Logs dragged out. The path had been destroyed, blocked by shake and stumps and churned-up dirt. David knew, roughly, that the trail should have gone straight, so he was sure he'd be able to pick it up on the other side of the clearing. He climbed over fallen branches and tripped and fell into them, the space underneath deeper than he thought. He gave up thirty feet in and turned around, dirty and with a small cut on his hand.

The walk back only took a few minutes. There was no one in the windows in the back of the house; he crossed the yard quickly and found the back door of the basement had locked after he closed it. He went around the side of the house, hoping to sneak in through the side door.

His aunt was in the driveway. She jumped and then said, "Thank God." She ran up and hugged David. She said, "Come in, everyone has been looking for you." At the door, she shouted up the stairs that she'd found him.

Everyone came to the stairs.

His dad said, "Where have you been?" His uncle, "What were you thinking?"

David's mom said, "He's back, let him be," and came down the stairs to hug him. "Where did you go?"

David said, "Just for a walk. I don't know. I was bored."

His uncle shook his head and said, "Not even a thought about how it would worry your parents?"

They had walked as a group to the living room. "It's okay," his mom said, "but you have to tell us where you are. We were worried."

David sat on the couch, and everyone looked at him, and then then they were looking over him, out the big bay window. He turned around and saw a police cruiser go by with its lights on. And then another. And another.

His mom had her hands over her mouth.

She said, "Oh my God she's on the mountain."

. . .

DAVID LEFT BECKY STANDING in the driveway and walked up the mountain. There were houses on both sides of the road now, but still no sidewalk, just a wide, grassy shoulder. He had only been up once since his sister went missing. When the first houses of phase one of the Mountainside had gone in, he'd been coming home from dinner with his mom and she said she wanted to take a quick look at what they were doing up there. They drove in silence, the newly paved road taking them past slash piles and foundation holes. Only a handful of houses had been completed.

The road rose gently for the first couple hundred metres before climbing. His sister ran this route almost every other night for three years. David had gone with her once, after his dad insisted he "do more than sit around and read comics" one night in grade nine. They ran slowly to the incline, past the gravel pit, then up to a steep hill to the gate, where they did stretches. They went back down to the bottom of the hill and turned around to head back up again. Laura would do sprints up, light jogs down, then bounds up, light jogs down. Twelve reps, up and down. David had done two reps with her, then sat on the gate and waited until she was done to head home together.

The road curved up slowly, toward where the gravel pit entrance had been.

James would be at the house soon. David would turn

over the box; there was no reason not to. Everything in it was available somewhere else. There was nothing new. He didn't have anything to add. Laura went for a run and didn't come back. A few days later, a trucker found her Discman on the logging roads. The people of Griffiths spent a week looking for her body. The story was always that same.

Where the road should have turned slightly to curve around the gravel pit, it instead ended in a cul-de-sac with two large concrete gateposts and half walls with "The Mountainside" spelled out in granite lettering. This was the back way into the subdivision and not as fancy as the main entrance off the old highway, which had small spotlights shining on the copper signs and a display of tulips.

David thought the entrance to the Mountainside was where the gravel pit gate had been when he was young, but it had changed so much he wasn't sure. The trees had all been cut down, and where the road should have gone on, up the mountain to the yellow gate, there was a driveway. He could see a shed, new trees planted over the road. He went into the Mountainside; the new road climbed steeply.

What could he add? He could tell James that he'd sat under the light while his dad was on the trail. He'd started to feel uncomfortable. The woods, dark and pressing in. The engine under him cooling and clicking and then silent. And then, a noise above him. Branches breaking, leaves being crushed. He thought a bear and then he thought about his sister and then his dad shouted, "Laura?" David's dad had walked the logging road around two switchbacks; rather than come back along the road, he cut straight down the mountainside. His flashlight moved shadows around David until he stepped out of the trees.

Could he tell how they got into the car and didn't speak on the way back down. How his mom was framed in the doorway by the light of the house. How she knew when they came back without her that Laura was not coming home. How she had called people all night despite knowing, asking if they'd seen Laura, at the same time she was being killed. That would fill in the story; a personal perspective. Humanizing. But it wouldn't change anything. It was still the same story.

The yards all had trees that were wrong for the mountain. Monkey puzzle trees, small shrubs, ornamental peach. The Douglas firs and sycamores had been cut down for terraced patches of lawn and tended yards. The roads in the Mountainside all seemed to branch off and fold back into the middle; all erratic loops leading up and down again. After two turns David was lost. A lot of the roads were just crescents or dead ends. Sometimes, the houses and trees would give way to a view, and he'd orient himself, but couldn't keep his bearings for more than a few minutes. He was sweating now, the sun shining right down on him. He got high enough to see the town and Fuller's Bay, across the valley. He took the next road that switched back, climbed up higher, grew tired from all the walking. At a playground, the water fountain didn't have water. A sign underneath told David water would be turned on May 1 each year. No one was at the playground; he had not seen anyone at all since he got into the subdivision. Probably, he thought, everyone was at work.

He could try to explain what he'd learned to James, but David wasn't sure he understood it himself. He hadn't had the words, before. When it happened to his sister. When people got killed here. When things happened over and over and people kept saying it wasn't that kind of place. David had known that wasn't true, but he hadn't known why. Carolyn knew. Staci knew. His mom knew. She had tried to tell James. But why would James understand what no reporter had before? He would just write the same story.

He would write of the town coming together. He would write of Becky's loyal friendship. He would write of the family's trauma. Of a father who had been unable to accept that the story had nothing to do with him. That an innocent man's life was ruined because of police mistakes. It would probably end with his mother, wishing her daughter had lived so she could have seen the mistakes she would have made — "It would have been nice to know," the mother said. And it would be a good story, David thought. Probably win James another award.

David passed, at last, a couple with a dog. They were on the other side of the street. The houses on that side were perched high up on purpose-built terraces. The ones on his left were down below him; he walked level with their second storeys, seeing into bedrooms. The couple asked if he was looking for something. He said, just walking. They were suspicious so he added, trying to find the entrance to the hiking trails. They gave him directions. They were not clear. Walk straight. Right on Mountain View Crescent, left on Valley View Lane. He forgot the words as they were said but thanked them and walked the way they had waved toward.

David had nothing to add. The box had nothing. He wouldn't hand over the diaries; they had nothing in them either, but they were private. The news footage had seemed like something but was nothing. James could have that. Maybe he could point out that David's dad hadn't actually found the body. But that would take away from the story. It would have to stay the same — Laura went for a run and didn't come back.

At the gate, she met someone. Someone waiting, in the bushes. Ready to grab her. David thought, No. That wasn't it. It would have been like Carolyn said. Just a thing that happened. The truck would have come down the logging road. She would have been cautious. Trucks came up and down the mountain. It wasn't that unusual, but it was night. It was dark. Maybe she thought it would be better to not be where she was, even while thinking she was being too cautious. But it was just as easy to leave. Maybe she started to head down. Why would she have stopped? The gate had been closed; a truck couldn't get around. She would have been able to get away if she thought she was in danger. They must have known her. Must have said her name. Said something to get her to stop. Someone from school? A thing that got out of hand. It just started as a joke. She would have told them to fuck off. Maybe one grabbed at her and she said she'd tell someone and then they knew they were in trouble. And if they were already in trouble, it wasn't too much farther to go. But that didn't seem right to David. Someone who knew her just happening to be there. It had to be someone who knew she would be there, waiting for her.

CHAPTER TWENTY-SIX

NEAR THE END OF a row of houses, walking along a rock face he was sure had been the edge of the gravel pit, he came to a turnoff road. A sign said "Trail Entrance." The road went up. There were no houses on it and David could see where it ended, at trees. A police car was parked there.

He walked toward it. A short street lamp, off now in daylight, hung above a yellow gate. The light over the gate was the same one he had sat under the night his sister went missing. The old logging road now a wide trail. A small shelter with a map of the area had been placed just to the side of the entrance. He walked toward it.

"Trail's closed." David recognized the cop who got out of the car.

He said, "Everything okay?"

"Can't say. We've got an investigation in progress." David waited. The cop said, "Body was found by some hikers. Other side of the mountain, by Robertson River. No way to know for sure but looks like suicide."

"Jesus."

"Hard to tell because a cougar or something got at it and pulled it down." He added, "There was a rope."

"Any idea who?"

"Nah. Looks like the body had been there a long time. The guy who found it wouldn't go near it. Always pulling bodies out of the woods here. Last year we had an old guy with Alzheimer's wandered up the mountain. Didn't find him for a month. Idiot hikers fell off the cliff a few years back. Some guy was missing fifteen years before they found him back there. He was probably killed, but hard to tell after fifteen years. Just yesterday I pulled a junkie out of the swamp."

"So much wilderness around here," David said. "I guess if you don't want to be found, it's a good place to go."

"Oh yeah, we probably don't find half of them. Remember that guy Farley? You might be too young. Crazy guy my uncle knew. Said he was in contact with aliens and then one day was just gone. Left a note that said he was going to rendezvous with them. They found bits of his truck way up on Pole Hill awhile back, but no body."

"My mom told me about him. He's a legend."

"For sure. Crazy as a bat. And then there was that girl back in the nineties. You're probably too young for that one, too. Whole town went looking for her."

"I remember."

"Yeah, it was big news. Never caught the guys who did it."

David said, "Guys?"

"Oh, fuck it, who knows? Might have been one guy. It was before my time, but you hear things."

"I thought," David said, "that some neighbour did it?"

"That's the story. But no one really buys that. They figure she got into something bad, got killed for it. Her mouth was filled with rocks."

David said, "Rocks?"

"That's what they do to rats. Kids getting in with the fucking bikers. Serves them right, you ask me."

A radio in his squad car crackled. He went to it. David nodded goodbye and walked back down the road.

Now that he had his bearings, it was easy to get home. He walked out the gates of the Mountainside and onto his road. Around the curve up ahead, he saw James's car. James stood in front of the door. He had rung the bell and was waiting. James took out his cell phone. He tapped the screen. He held it to his ear and then he turned and saw David.

ACKNOWLEDGEMENTS

Thank you to my family: Daniella Balabuk, Eliot, and Charlie. To my mom, Edna Melgaard. To Jodi Mason, for early reading. To Marilyn Biderman, for taking care of the business side of things. To House of Anansi — my editor, Doug Richmond, publisher Leigh Nash, Michelle MacAleese, Jenny McWha, Erica Mojzes, and Debby de Groot. To Linda Pruessen, for copy edits. And to the Ontario Arts Council and to the Canada Council for the Arts for the grants that made the book possible.

MICHAEL MELGAARD is the author of the short story collection *Pallbearing*. His writing has appeared in *Best Canadian Stories* anthology, as well as *Joyland*, *Lithub*, and elsewhere. Originally from Vancouver Island, he currently lives in Toronto.